T0284085

PUMPKIN
SPICE PUPPY

Books by Laurien Berenson

Melanie Travis Mysteries

A PEDIGREE TO DIE FOR
UNDERDOG
DOG EAT DOG
HAIR OF THE DOG
WATCHDOG
HUSH PUPPY
UNLEASHED
ONCE BITTEN
HOT DOG
BEST IN SHOW
JINGLE BELL BARK
RAINING CATS AND DOGS
CHOW DOWN
HOUNDED TO DEATH
DOGGIE DAY CARE MURDER
GONE WITH THE WOOF
DEATH OF A DOG WHISPERER
THE BARK BEFORE CHRISTMAS
LIVE AND LET GROWL
MURDER AT THE PUPPY FEST
WAGGING THROUGH THE SNOW
RUFF JUSTICE
BITE CLUB
HERE COMES SANTA PAWS
GAME OF DOG BONES
HOWLOWEEN MURDER
PUP FICTION
SHOW ME THE BUNNY
KILLER CUPID
PUMPKIN SPICE PUPPY

A Senior Sleuths Mystery

PEG AND ROSE SOLVE A MURDER
PEG AND ROSE STIR UP TROUBLE
PEG AND ROSE PLAY THE PONIES

Published by Kensington Publishing Corp.

Laurien Berenson

PUMPKIN SPICE PUPPY

A Melanie Travis Canine Mystery

Kensington Publishing Corp.
www.kensingtonbooks.com

KENSINGTON BOOKS are published by

Kensington Publishing Corp.
900 Third Avenue
New York, NY 10022

All Kensington titles, imprints and distributed lines are available at special quantity discounts for bulk purchases for sales promotion, premiums, fund-raising, educational or institutional use. Special book excerpts or customized printings can also be created to fit specific needs. For details, write or phone the office of the Kensington Special Sales Manager: Kensington Publishing Corp., 900 Third Ave., New York, NY, 10022. Attn. Special Sales Department. Phone: 1-800-221-2647.

KENSINGTON and the KENSINGTON COZIES teapot logo Reg. US Pat. & TM Off.

Library of Congress Control Number: 2024936523

ISBN: 978-1-4967-5062-4

First Kensington Hardcover Edition: September 2024

ISBN: 978-1-4967-5064-8 (ebook)

10 9 8 7 6 5 4 3 2 1

Printed in the United States of America

PUMPKIN SPICE PUPPY

Chapter One

Nothing gets my family out of bed faster on a Sunday morning than the prospect of spending the day at a dog show. I'd like to think that our lives don't entirely revolve around dogs, but since we have five of them and there are four of us, it's a close call.

Four of the five are black Standard Poodles, all retired show dogs, now living their best lives as much-loved companions. The last is Bud, a small spotted dog of unknown origin, found on the side of the road by my older son, Davey. As opposed to the Poodles, who are perfectly behaved, Bud is a wild man who makes his own rules. It's a good thing that little trouble-maker is cute.

Davey is fifteen and a sophomore in high school, so he likes to think he makes his own rules too. In the past year, he's shot past me in height. Now his body is all lanky limbs and sharp angles. Once he gets moving, however, Davey is surprisingly graceful. That will help today. The reason my family was on our way to a dog show was because Davey was entered to handle a Standard Poodle who belonged to my Aunt Peg.

"We've been driving forever," a voice piped up from the back seat of the SUV. "Why aren't we there yet?"

Five years old, Kevin was a blond-haired, blue-eyed replica of my husband, Sam. Kev possessed many wonderful qualities, but patience wasn't one of them. We'd been on the road for an hour, so it wasn't a surprise that he was tired of sitting still.

"Your timing is excellent," Sam said as a large building loomed into view. "We're about to turn into the parking lot."

It's hard for me to believe Sam and I have been married for seven years. Sometimes it feels as though we've known each other forever. Other times, it seems like the years have passed in the blink of an eye. Sam says the luckiest day of his life was the day he and I met. I think he has that backward. I'm definitely the one who's been lucky.

The four of us had spent the past six months participating in dog shows that were held outdoors in lovely parks or open, grassy fields. Now it was the first week of November. In Connecticut, that meant there was frost on the ground and a winter chill in the air. Also that the dog show circuit had moved inside until spring.

The good thing about the change in venues was

that exhibitors wouldn't have to worry about poor footing, inclement weather, or fading light. The bad: a dozen show rings and a thousand dogs, plus their crates, grooming tables, blow-dryers, and other assorted supplies would all be crammed together in very close quarters.

Fortunately for us, Aunt Peg would have arrived early and have already dealt with some of those problems. A relative by marriage, Peg was a woman in her seventies with a formidable intellect. Having spent decades producing some of the best Standard Poodles in the country, Aunt Peg was now a distinguished dog show judge. She had a direct gaze, forceful opinions, and a work ethic that would put a longshoreman to shame.

There was nothing Aunt Peg admired more than useful people, and she'd done her best to force me into that mold. Her standards were high, and her expectations higher still. I wasn't the only person who sometimes struggled to measure up.

During the previous year, Davey had handled Aunt Peg's homebred bitch, Cedar Crest Coral, to her championship. Now Peg was considering the possibility of a specials career—entering her to compete against other champions for Group and Best in Show wins—for Coral. Aunt Peg hoped Davey would want to continue handling the Poodle.

We were all there to give the idea a trial run.

Sam parked the SUV, then we entered the building and went straight to the crowded grooming room, where the pre-ring preparations would take place. I scanned the cavernous space and saw that Aunt Peg had secured a spot for her crate and grooming table beside the setup belonging to professional handler, Crawford Langley, and his assistant and husband, Terry Denunzio. Coral was standing on the tabletop beside her

"Over here!" Aunt Peg called out, waving a hand above her head. As one of the taller people in the room, she was already hard to miss.

"I see Aunt Peg," Kevin cried eagerly. He dropped my hand and ran on ahead.

"We *all* see her," I muttered. "And I think half the room heard her."

Sam reached over and gave me a warning poke. He knows that my relationship with Aunt Peg has always been complicated. His, meanwhile, is utterly straightforward. Sam's a huge fan. His stride lengthened as he went to greet Peg with a smile.

If only it were that easy for me.

"We're not late," I said as we approached. Davey had hurried to the other side of the setup. He was already unpacking Peg's tack box and lining up a row of grooming tools along the edge of Coral's table.

Aunt Peg's brow rose. "Did I say you were?"

"No, but you were thinking it."

A snicker came from next door. Terry, no doubt. I hadn't even had a chance to say hello and he was already having fun at my expense.

Terry was a few years younger than me and drop dead gorgeous, a fact that was wasted on, well, pretty much everyone, since he only had eyes for Crawford. A longtime couple, they'd tied the knot on Valentine's Day, and we'd all been there to celebrate with them. Terry's hairstyle changed as often as his mood. Today his locks were blond and curled softly around his ears. Though he looked as innocent as a Renaissance cherub, I wasn't fooled for a minute.

I turned and blew an air-kiss in his direction. "Cut that out, mister. Or you won't be my favorite person in the room anymore."

"Hey!" said Sam. He was down near the floor, helping Kevin unpack the bag of toys he'd brought with him.

"Hey!" Davey echoed in mock outrage.

"Hey!" Kevin chimed in, not because he understood what was going on, but because he hated to be left out.

My family had a point.

"Okay, fourth favorite," I said to Terry. "But that's still pretty good, right?"

He cast a glance Aunt Peg's way in case she wanted

to object. She'd sidled over to stand beside Davey and was pretending to be oblivious. Probably a lucky thing under the circumstances.

"Close enough." Terry flashed me a cheeky grin. "I'll take it. Crawford's over at the MinPin ring, but he'll be back shortly. He wants to talk to you about offering a prize."

"Sure," I replied without thinking. "Wait . . . what?"

"A prize. For your thingie."

That explanation didn't help.

"Yes, of course. My thingie," I repeated. "I've been worried about that all day." Davey was trying not to laugh. I hated to think what my teenage son might be imagining. "Terry, what are we talking about?"

"You know." He fluttered a hand in the air. "Your school thing."

I stared at him blankly.

"Oh for Pete's sake," said Aunt Peg. "The Howard Academy fundraiser. Surely it hasn't slipped your mind. You've been talking about it for a month."

Oh, *that.*

During the week, I worked half days as a special needs tutor at a private school in Greenwich, Connecticut. Howard Academy was a select institution, catering to both children of privilege and scholarship students, and providing a stellar education to all. The school's primary goal was to provide a solid foundation upon which our graduating eighth-graders would base the rest of their academic careers.

That level of excellence couldn't be maintained on a budget, however. HA had been founded a century earlier in a mansion donated by benefactors Joshua and Honoria Howard. Now the building was showing its age, and growing enrollment over the years had necessitated the addition of two new wings. Not only that, but attracting the best teachers also meant paying a premium for them.

Howard Academy had managed for decades on the proceeds from a generous endowment. Now those halcyon days were waning. The school's finances were far from dire, but its board believed in planning ahead.

Other school principals might have proposed a bake sale or car wash. Not our esteemed headmaster, Russell Hanover II. As usual, he was thinking bigger.

The result was that his assistant, Harriet Bloom, and I had spent the previous month ironing out the details of his Thanks for Giving fundraiser.

"It's my day off," I said. Even to my own ears, my words sounded plaintive and maybe a little whiney. "I shouldn't have to think about work."

"Pish." Aunt Peg snorted. Beside her, Davey had Coral lying on her side on the rubber-matted table-top. She was overseeing his line-brushing of the Poodle's dense mane coat. "The fundraiser isn't supposed to be work. You described it as a treasure hunt."

"It is." I brightened at the thought. Harriet and I had come up with the theme together. I thought it was genius. "We're getting the students involved in raising money for the school by sending them on a quest."

Terry also had a Standard Poodle out on his grooming table. He was busy layering hairspray through the dog's copious topknot. Now he paused to waggle his eyebrows. "What kind of quest? Please tell me it involves swords and dragons."

"Nope," said Kevin. He was running a matchbox car around the floor of Coral's crate. Since he was in kindergarten at Howard Academy, his class was taking part in the treasure hunt. "This one is about pumpkin spice muffins."

"You're kidding." Terry laughed.

"I wish." Kev sighed.

"I like pumpkin spice muffins," Sam mentioned.

"As do I," Aunt Peg agreed. That wasn't a surprise. She had a ferocious sweet tooth.

"It's only the tokens that are shaped like muffins," Davey told his little brother. "Once you collect enough of them, you can turn them in for prizes."

Kevin looked up at him. "What kinds of prizes?"

I was sure his teacher had already briefed his class on the possibilities, but I was happy to elaborate anyway. "There are lots of great things to choose from. Toys, games, sporting equipment, gift certificates, even a motorized scooter. One parent offered a ski weekend at their chalet in Vermont. And more donations are arriving every day."

"That's where Crawford comes in," Terry said. "He wants to donate a prize too."

"That's very generous. I'll talk to him about it after the judging." I paused, struck by a sudden thought. "How did Crawford know about the fundraiser?"

"How do you think?" Aunt Peg asked as Davey set his brushes aside and nudged Coral to stand up and shake out her coat. "I told him. I was quite certain his skills would be much in demand." Peg, a Howard Academy alumna, had already offered several prizes of her own.

"Who's in demand?" Crawford asked, striding back into the setup with a Miniature Pinscher tucked beneath his arm and a purple-and-gold Best of Breed rosette clutched in his hand. He was a dapper man in his late sixties—astute, dignified, and always impeccably turned out. Crawford had been at the pinnacle of the dog show game for as long as Peg had. Like her, he had no intention of retiring anytime soon.

"You are," I said.

Crawford chuckled. "Like that's news."

He handed the small dog to Terry, who slipped it inside one of the stacked crates that bordered their setup. Having won its breed, the MinPin would compete again later in the Toy Group.

"Aunt Peg's helping," Kevin said. Now that the conversation had turned to prizes, he'd forgotten all about his toy cars.

"I always help," she pointed out.

That was a matter of opinion. One I had no intention of voicing aloud.

Then Sam caught my eye and grinned, and I had to bite back a laugh. Spousal shorthand. After all these years, he knew exactly what I was thinking.

"Maybe you'd like to help me spray up Coral," Davey invited.

While we'd been talking, he'd put in the bitch's topknot. The long hair, currently unsprayed, was listing to one side. Given a comb and a can of hairspray, Aunt Peg could take care of that problem in a jiff. Come to think of it, so could Davey. Usually he preferred to do all of Coral's pre-ring prep himself. I wondered why this time was different.

So I asked.

"Umm . . ." Davey might be a teenager, but I knew he could do better than that. I waited for him to make another attempt.

"Don't mind me." Never one to turn down an opportunity, Aunt Peg was already stepping around him to take charge.

"Coral's a special now," Davey said.

"Yes, she is." We all knew that.

"So the stakes are higher, and she needs to look perfect. Plus, I haven't shown her since last summer—"

"Oh for Pete's sake," Aunt Peg interrupted, casting a glare my way. "Don't browbeat the poor boy. Davey, put on your jacket. Do you have bait in your pocket? No? Then hurry up and remedy that. And comb your hair while you're at it. Look at Crawford's dog. He's ready to head to the ring, which means we need to be too."

Comb and fingers flying, Aunt Peg finished the job with a flourish. She set the can of hairspray down on the tabletop and kissed Coral on the nose. Then she looked around at Sam, Davey, Kevin, and me. We were all standing there staring at her.

"What?" she demanded.

"Nothing," I replied.

"That's what I thought." Aunt Peg gave the Poodle's coat one final tweak, then hopped her down from the table. In the setup next door, Crawford was about to leave. We'd be right behind him. Peg unspooled Coral's narrow show leash and handed it to Davey.

"Smile," she said to him. "It's time for both of you to shine."

Chapter
Two

Terry went first to clear a path though the crowded room. Crawford followed with his Standard Poodle. Coral was behind them, with Sam, Aunt Peg, and Davey forming an honor guard around the perfectly coiffed Poodle so no one could reach out and touch her. Kevin and I brought up the rear.

The dog show was part of a "Fall Festival Cluster," and the hall where the event was held had been decorated to reflect the theme. We walked past a stack of hay bales topped by a row of jack-o'-lanterns. Arrangements of marigolds and chrysanthemums adorned the show rings. When we came to a stuffed scarecrow with button eyes and a floppy straw hat, Kevin abruptly stopped and stared.

"What is *that?*" he asked.

"You've seen a scarecrow before. We watched *The Wizard of Oz* together."

Kev leaned in for a closer look. "Is he alive?"

I quickly stifled a laugh. "No. The scarecrow in the movie wasn't really alive either. It was just make believe."

He considered that as I tugged on his hand to get him moving again. We needed to get to the ring. The Standard Poodle judging was about to start, and the entry wasn't large. That was one of the reasons Aunt Peg had chosen this show for Coral's first venture in Best of Variety competition.

Usually Crawford would have had a special of his own to show. Today he'd brought just one Standard Poodle with him—the class dog. Even so, I wasn't about to get my hopes up. Crawford always had to be considered a threat. He was perfectly capable of beating Davey from the classes.

"What about the Tin Man?" Kevin asked, as we hurried to catch up.

"No. Sorry." I glanced down. "He was a made-up character, too. They all were."

"*Even the Wizard?*" His voice rose in stunned disbelief as we arrived at ringside. Several exhibitors, waiting their turns outside the gate, turned to look.

Sam appeared beside us. He'd picked up Davey's numbered armband from the steward. The Puppy Dog class was already being judged.

"Everything okay?" he asked as he affixed the number to the top of Davey's sleeve.

"Fine," I told him. "We're just having a small *Wizard of Oz* crisis."

Eyes trained on the competition, Aunt Peg said under her breath, "As long as it isn't a Poodle crisis, it can wait."

"Don't worry, munchkin." Davey reached over and ruffled his brother's hair. Of the five of us standing there grouped around Coral, he appeared to be the most composed. "We'll fix your problem when I come out of the ring."

No one was surprised when Crawford's Poodle won the Open Dog class, then beat the winner of the Puppy class, taking the award of Winners Dog and the points toward his championship that came with it. Just four class bitches were entered. The judge took less than ten minutes to sort them out and pick his Winners Bitch. Then it was Davey and Coral's turn.

The Best of Variety competition consisted of Coral, two additional champion bitches, Crawford's Winners Dog and the Winners Bitch. When the five Poodles were lined up along one side of the ring—the three champions in front, followed by the class dogs—we all moved in closer so we wouldn't miss a thing.

I quickly realized Davey was the only nonprofessional handler in the class. In his place, I'd have been nervous. Davey looked cool, calm, and very competent. He and Coral were second in the row, but Davey paid no attention to the champions on either side of him. He simply did his job and concentrated on his own Poodle. He stacked Coral in a square stance, with her head and tail up. Then he waited for the judge to make his first pass down the line.

Having concluded his duties for the time being, Terry came over to stand beside us. While the judge ran his gaze over the group of Poodles in the ring, Terry did the same.

"Coral looks good in there," he said softly.

"Shhh!" Aunt Peg hissed. She was wildly superstitious when it came to predictions about the judging.

Terry just shrugged. He was one of the few people who wasn't intimidated by her. "I'm only saying what I see."

"Don't make me cover your mouth," Aunt Peg growled.

Terry grinned. "I'd like to see you try." His voice was lower still this time. Even he didn't dare provoke Peg twice at ringside.

Then the judge motioned for the handlers to take their Poodles around the ring together and we all went silent. Even Kevin appeared to be mesmerized by the sight. Coral's movement was breathtaking. It was one of the reasons Davey had been able to successfully handle her to her championship. It definitely caught the judge's eye on the first go-around.

Then his gaze slid past Coral and landed on Crawford's dog. Not only was the big black Poodle a superior specimen of the breed, he also possessed the advantage of having Crawford at the end of his leash. The dog was striding around the ring as if he owned the place.

"That's trouble," Sam murmured.

"Indeed." Aunt Peg sighed.

Terry and I shared a look. We'd both seen the same thing they had.

The judge placed the two dogs on one side of the ring, then turned the competition into a duel among the trio of champion bitches. Briefly that made me hope that he planned to choose his Best of Variety winner from among them. Davey did a commendable job of presenting Coral, and the bitch herself was lovely. Of these three, she was clearly the best.

Unfortunately that wasn't enough. When the judge made his final decision, he motioned Crawford's dog to the top spot. Coral was placed behind him. The judge then pointed and announced his winners. Best of Variety and Best of Winners to the big black dog in front. Best of Opposite Sex to Coral.

"Oh well," Aunt Peg said. She shrugged and turned away.

"Oh well," Kevin echoed as Davey accepted the red-and-white rosette from the judge, then exited the ring. Crawford and his Poodle remained behind to have his picture taken. Terry hurried in to help make repairs to the dog's coat.

"I'm sorry," Davey told Aunt Peg, when he and Coral reached the spot where we'd gathered to watch.

"Are you?" She gazed down at him and arched a brow. "For what?"

"For not winning," he said unhappily. "I tried hard. Coral did too. I thought she looked great."

"She did," Peg agreed.

"But . . ." Davey began.

"But," Aunt Peg interrupted him firmly, "you were so busy concentrating on your own dog that you didn't take a moment to evaluate your competition."

Davey looked surprised. "That's the judge's job."

"Of course. But it's also yours. It's not enough just to know your own dog's merits and flaws. When you're in the ring, you also need to know what you're up against. What good does it do to showcase your Poodle's pretty head if the Poodle standing behind you has an even prettier one?"

Davey didn't say a word. He'd obviously never considered that.

"Just because the dog that beat you today came from the classes, doesn't mean he wasn't worthy of respect in the Variety ring. If you'd been paying more attention, you'd have realized what a handsome Standard Poodle Crawford had in there. That dog will be a special himself soon enough—and then we'll all need to watch out. Even on Coral's best day, he's more than capable of giving her a run for her money."

Davey frowned. He still didn't look happy. "I guess so."

Aunt Peg wasn't finished. "There's no reason for you to exit the ring and stand around moping," she added briskly. "Of course you wanted to win. I wanted to win too. But you have to keep an open mind and realize that you don't always deserve to."

Kevin must have realized that his brother was on the losing end of that discussion because he marched over to stand in front of Aunt Peg. He tipped back his head and stared way up at her. "I wanted to win too," he announced.

"Did you?" She gazed down at him. "Why?"

"Because I like purple-and-gold ribbons."

"If you're lucky, maybe next time we'll get one for you. But now your parents and I are going to take Coral back to the setup. Perhaps you and Davey should take a few minutes to work out your wizard problems. Then we'll see you back there shortly?"

Aunt Peg posed the remark as a question, but we all knew we'd been given our orders. As we headed back toward the grooming area, I fell in beside her.

"Did you mean what you told Davey back there?" I asked.

"Of course I did."

"All of it?"

This time she hesitated.

"Is Crawford's dog better than Coral? Would you have marked that class the same way?"

"No, not today," Aunt Peg admitted. "But it was close. And I can see how someone else might compare the two and place them differently than I would."

"Not to mention the Crawford factor," Sam said. "Davey did well showing Coral in the classes, but if he wants to be competitive showing in the Variety against the pros, he's going to have to take his skills up a notch."

Aunt Peg nodded in agreement. "You're quite right. The margin for error is growing slimmer all the time. We're in the big leagues now."

Chapter
Three

Mondays start early at my house. Two kids, two jobs, and five dogs are a lot to manage. Sam mostly handles his part with aplomb. I'm the one who's likely to be running around the house at the last minute looking for lost homework or missing shoes.

Whatever problems crop up, Bud is usually the guilty party. Somehow he manages to take up more bandwidth than all our Standard Poodles combined. Faith is our oldest Poodle and my best friend. She and I have been together for nine years, and the bond we share is incredibly meaningful. Her delightful daughter, Eve, is our other female Poodle. The two males are Tar and Augie. Tar is a loveable goofball, and Augie is Davey's dog. Davey raised Augie and trained him. Augie sleeps on Davey's bed, just as Bud sleeps with Kevin.

Sam works from home, so his morning routine is

less hectic. At least it feels that way to me. Together, he and I make sure that the boys are dressed and fed and the dogs are fed and exercised. Then Davey takes the bus to the local high school. After that, Kevin, Faith, and I carpool to Howard Academy.

Once there, our first stop is at Miss Wheeler's kindergarten room to drop off Kevin. Then Faith and I hurry through the mansion to the passageway that leads to the new wing where my classroom is located. We're supposed to be checked in and presentable by eight-thirty. Faith and I nearly always make it on time.

That morning was destined to be one of those days when we didn't.

Faith and I were racing along an interior corridor when I was hailed from the mansion's front hall. Harriet Bloom, the headmaster's assistant, was at her post outside Mr. Hanover's office door. "Melanie, do you have a minute?"

I skidded to a stop so quickly that Faith flew right past me. The Poodle tapped on the brakes, then doubled back to join me.

"Of course, Harriet." I quickly changed course. "What do you need?"

The older woman seated behind the desk looked harmless. But behind Harriet's plump cheeks, twinset sweaters, and tasteful pearls lay the will of a Pit Bull. Her tenure at Howard Academy was rumored to be numbered in decades, rather than mere years. She was smart, practical, and hard-working, and Russell Hanover was fortunate to have her acting as his gate-keeper.

Harriet and I had organized the Thanksgiving fund-raiser together. In the process, we'd discovered that we make a great team. The treasure hunt had begun the previous week. I assumed she wanted to give me an update on how the event was proceeding.

Faith was at my side when I entered the spacious front hall. Its two-story vaulted ceiling, polished hardwood floor, and heritage furniture were meant to impress even the most discerning parents. They were also a deliberate nod to the building's storied past. Portraits of the school's founders stared down at me from above a sideboard. A seasonal arrangement of gourds, displayed in a woven basket, decorated a round table in the middle of the room.

Another time, I might have taken a moment to appreciate the room's ambience. Now, however, Harriet was waiting for me. She opened a desk drawer and pulled out a dog biscuit for Faith as we approached.

"What's up?" I said.

Harriet led with a pleased smile. "Donations, for starters. Not only that, but tokens are pouring in."

"Good for us?" It seemed too early in the process to begin celebrating, though maybe a small fist bump was warranted. I held up my hand. Harriet just stared at it.

"Moving on," she said. "At the moment, our sixth-graders are leading the way. Eighth grade is in second spot." She peered at the numbers on the screen in front of her. "Some of the younger grades need to step it up."

I took the biscuit from Harriet and handed it to Faith. She lay down on the floor to eat it. "They will," I said. "Don't forget that the little kids can't run around town on their own. They're dependent upon parents, or maybe a nanny, to help them out. That may take some time to organize."

Russell Hanover's vision for the fundraiser was a treasure hunt that took place in Howard Academy's hometown of Greenwich. Local shops had made donations, which earned them a supply of tokens—shaped like pumpkin spice muffins—to hide in and around their premises. Students were eager to hunt down the tokens since they could be turned in for prizes at the end of the event.

Participating stores benefitted not only from the school's substantial PR campaign, but also the increase in foot traffic. Our students were more than happy to shop while they searched, and so far, all the feedback we'd received had been positive.

It was my idea to have school parents act as sponsors, pledging a sum for each token collected by students in a child's grade. As an added incentive, the grade whose students turned in the highest number of tokens would be awarded an extra vacation day on the Monday after Thanksgiving—a boon for families that would be traveling for the holiday.

"So that's the good news," Harriet said.

Something in her tone alerted me. Apparently it *was* too early to begin patting ourselves on the back.

"Does that mean there's bad news?" I asked carefully.

"I'm not sure, but I'd like you to find out. There's been a complaint from one of the participating stores." Harriet picked up a note from her desk and read off the name. "Willet's Pet Supplies. Are you familiar with it?"

"Yes."

Harriet glanced at Faith. "I thought you might be."

Considering how many dogs we had to feed, I was familiar with just about every pet supply option in lower Fairfield County. My family lived in the neighboring town of Stamford so I didn't shop there often, but I remembered Mr. Willet as an amiable man.

"What was the complaint about?" I asked curiously.

"Unfortunately, I don't know. The call came in after hours yesterday, and Mr. Willet didn't leave a detailed message." Harriet handed me the paper. "I'm sure he expects us to get back to him. Do you have time to check on it this morning?"

"Sure. My first tutoring session starts in"—I

glanced at my watch—"yikes, about one minute. But I have a break between eleven-fifteen and noon. I'll get in touch with him then."

I nudged Faith to her feet. Before we could leave, Harriet reached out a hand to stop me. "One more thing. Whatever the problem turns out to be, don't make a fuss. Just *fix it*. This fundraiser is Mr. Hanover's pet project. You and I both know we can't allow anything to go wrong."

"I'll do my best," I promised.

When we reached my classroom, I turned on the lights, hung up my coat, and tucked my purse into a desk drawer, then took a minute to catch my breath. Faith went straight to her bed in the corner and lay down. Both of us attempted to look as though we hadn't just arrived in a hurry. We probably didn't fool anyone.

Students came to my classroom for a variety of reasons. Most were referred for tutoring by their teachers. Occasionally, one would just show up and ask for help. Howard Academy prided itself on its rigorous academic standards. Some kids exceled under that kind of pressure, while others struggled not to fall behind. A few gave up entirely.

Parents often assumed that my job was to ensure their children earned the grades required for acceptance at an exclusive prep school. I disagreed. My duty was to teach their children to think, to allow them to ask questions, and to offer whatever kind of support was needed. Sometimes it was as simple as convincing a student that he or she belonged at Howard Academy and was capable of doing the work.

My first tutoring session was with a second-grader who was learning to cope with dyslexia. In the next, I helped a sixth-grader who thought she was hopeless at math complete her algebra homework. By eleven-ten, the room was empty again.

I took out my phone and called the number Mr. Willet had left. After three rings, an answering machine picked up. I disconnected the call without leaving a message. Considering that he was already unhappy with us, it would probably be better if I made the effort to talk to Mr. Willet in person.

Howard Academy wasn't far from downtown Greenwich. Willet's Pet Supplies, on Putnam Avenue, was scarcely more than a mile away. Faith and I should be able to easily make it to the store and back before my next tutoring session was due to begin.

"What do you think?" I turned to ask Faith's opinion. She immediately jumped to her feet. Even though I hadn't specified the nature of my query, she was always up for an adventure.

I went and got my coat. Faith's leash was in the pocket. Her pomponned tail whipped back and forth as I clipped it to her collar. A morning break usually meant a cup of coffee at my desk. Faith was definitely in favor of this change in routine.

She and I hurried down the quiet hallway between the rows of classrooms. A flight of stairs at the end took us down to the ground floor, where a fire door was always left unlocked for safety. Faith and I exited together on the side of the building.

Howard Academy's campus was set on twenty acres of beautiful land. Some of it was wooded, but there were meadows too. From where we stood, high on a slope, I could see the school's soccer and lacrosse fields spread out below us.

Faith and I set off at a brisk pace, the Poodle dancing at the end of her leash. The crisp fall air felt wonderful, it was just cold enough to sting my cheeks. Treetops displayed a beautiful array of colors. Fallen leaves cracked beneath my boots. Faith looked amused when I dragged my feet, then kicked a pile of leaves high in the air.

We angled down the hill and across the large front lawn, emerging nearly at the end of the school's lengthy driveway. I hoped Mr. Hanover was busy at his desk rather than watching our escape through his office window. Or that Harriet would cover for us, if it came to that.

A quarter mile later, Faith and I arrived at a sidewalk. The Post Road's business district began shortly after that. Faith was still trotting along happily. I had a blister beginning to form on my heel and was wishing I'd thought to change into a pair of sneakers before we set out. Luckily, we didn't have much farther to go. I could see Willet's red-and-white sign at the end of the next block.

Unlike the fancy shops and boutiques that lined the rest of the road, Mr. Willet's store was a simple concrete block building, square in shape and unadorned by unnecessary frills or decorations. Even its color was plain: a shade of white so bright that it reflected the sun.

There was a small parking lot between the pet supply store and the hair salon next door. It offered just four spaces, and all of them were full. The vehicles were luxury sedans that looked more likely to belong to patrons of the salon rather than Mr. Willet's store.

As Faith and I approached the entrance, I was pleased to see that Mr. Willet had a copy of our colorful poster—designed by Howard Academy art students—affixed to his front window. "THANKS FOR GIVING" was written across the top in vibrant red-and-gold script. The middle featured a silhouette of Joshua Howard's mansion against a leafy background. A row of pumpkin spice tokens danced across the bottom of the poster, decorating an additional line of script. "WE APPRECIATE YOUR HELP!"

As I stopped to admire the students' handiwork, Faith lifted her nose and sniffed the air. The store stocked all kinds of dog treats and large bags of kibble. That was probably what she smelled. I pushed the glass door open, and a bell tinkled softly to announce our arrival.

Late morning on a Monday, the store was quiet. From where we stood, just inside the door, its aisles appeared to be empty. Even so, I was surprised not to hear Mr. Willet call out his usual cheery greeting.

"Let's take a look around," I said to Faith. "Maybe he's in the storeroom."

Faith's ears flattened against the sides of her head. She whined softly under her breath. One of those reactions would have been enough to make me pause. Both at the same time raised the hair on the back of my neck.

"What's the matter?" I said. For some reason, I was whispering now.

That didn't matter to Faith. She had no trouble hearing me. She turned her head and gazed toward a hallway at the back of the store. Now that I was paying attention, I could hear the faint sound that must have caught her attention.

Thump! Thump! Thump!

I frowned, perplexed. "What *is* that?"

Faith didn't know either. But she definitely didn't like it. Nor did I.

"Something's wrong," I said, already hurrying toward the source of the sound. Faith scrambled to keep up. "I hope Mr. Willet's all right."

We reached the back of the store and stopped at the entrance to the short hallway. The sound was louder there. Then, abruptly, it ceased. Faith began to growl under her breath.

I'd never heard her do that before. I wished I wasn't hearing it now.

There were two doors, one on either side of the hall. The one labeled "STOREROOM" was closed. The other had a small sign that identified it as Mr. Willet's office. That door was cracked open a couple of inches. From where we stood, I couldn't see inside.

Faith's body stiffened. She began to back away from the office door, not stopping until the leash was taut between us. Clearly she wished I would follow. I really wanted to take Faith's advice, but I couldn't run away when there was a chance that Mr. Willet might need our help.

Instead, I dropped the leash and took a cautious step toward the partially open door. Then I leaned forward and peered inside the room. The interior was dark and cluttered. Even so, one brief glimpse was enough to show me all I needed to know. Faith's instincts had been spot-on.

Mr. Willet was slumped over his desk with a knife protruding from his back. There was nothing I could do for him. He was beyond our help now.

Chapter Four

I might have screamed at the gruesome sight. I don't actually remember. I do know that Faith immediately began to bark.

As soon as she did that, the thumping noise resumed. It was coming from behind me now. After a moment, it was joined by a deep-throated howl.

Suddenly, the sound Faith and I had been hearing made sense.

Mr. Willet owned a Chow Chow named Cider. The dog often accompanied him to the store. Faith and Cider had even met once. I knew that Chows could be fierce when they wanted to be. They also tended to be very protective of their owners.

Whoever attacked Willet must have realized that he needed to get Cider out of the way. He'd taken the precaution to lock the Chow in the storeroom. Sensing that something terrible was happening, the poor dog must have been throwing his body against the door, trying to get out, ever since.

Much as I felt sorry for Cider, I didn't dare touch the door now. Instead I began to backpedal quickly down the hallway, then through the rest of the store. This time, Faith was only too happy to accompany me. She and I didn't stop moving until we were outside on the sidewalk.

Though we were standing in the sun, I felt like I was freezing. My hands were shaking so badly I could hardly get my phone out of my pocket. I wasted too much time before finally managing to call 9-1-1. Thankfully, once I'd told my story to the dispatcher, he assured me that police were on the way.

My legs were quivering too. Indeed, it felt as though my whole body was trembling. I sank down onto the sidewalk, then moved over to sit with my back braced against the store's concrete wall. When I patted my knees, Faith climbed in my lap. She felt warm and solid. I hugged her to me, and Faith leaned into the caress. I buried my face in her thick curls.

Together, we waited for help to come.

It took six minutes for the first police cruiser to arrive. I know because I spent most of that time concentrating on the nearly imperceptible movement of the hands on my watch. It was better than thinking about what I'd seen inside the store.

A single officer got out and looked at me quizzically. "Ma'am, did you report finding a body?"

I nodded. Then pointed. "In the office toward the rear of the building. But whatever you do, don't open the storeroom door."

As he stepped past Faith and me and entered the building, another police car pulled up to join the first. This one held two officers. One went inside the pet supply store. The second remained on the sidewalk with me.

This officer was short and stocky. His blue uniform was neatly pressed and fit like a glove. His name tag identified him as Officer Prudhoe. He stood with his thumbs hooked in the top of his belt and gazed at me like there were a lot of questions he wanted to ask.

Given that, it was unnerving that he didn't say a word.

The sight of two police cruisers on the road out front was enough to bring people out of the salon next door to see what was going on. Now that a crowd was gathering, I needed to stand up. I gave Faith one last grateful squeeze, then shifted her off my lap.

On the first attempt, my legs wobbled as if they might not hold me. Officer Prudhoe reached out. His hand circled my arm with a firm grasp. He held on until I was steady on my feet.

"You don't look so good," he said. "Do you think you're going to throw up?"

I pulled in a deep breath. "No."

"Good." He nodded. "You want a bottle of water?"

"No, thank you."

"Your dog." Prudhoe nodded in Faith's direction. Obligingly, she wagged her tail in response. He didn't seem to notice. "She doesn't bite, does she?"

"No. Never." I pulled her in close to my side, in case he had an idea that she didn't belong there. "And she's current on all her shots."

"Also good to know," he said.

While I waited to see what would happen next, I gave Harriet a quick call. Noon was approaching fast. There was no way I'd be back at school in time for the two tutoring sessions I had scheduled before my work day ended at one o'clock.

"Something's come up," I told her in a voice hardly louder than a whisper. Standing three feet away, Officer Prudhoe wasn't even pretending not to listen to the conversation. "You're going to have to cancel my classes."

"Melanie, what—?"

"Sorry, I can't explain now. I have to go."

"Just tell me one thing," Harrier insisted. "Are you all right?"

There were a dozen different ways I could have answered that question. None of them would have been reassuring. "Sort of," I said finally. "I'll explain everything later."

"Classes?" Prudhoe asked when I'd put the phone away.

"Yes, I work at . . ." My voice trailed away. Belatedly it occurred to me that if the police contacted the school, Mr. Hanover wasn't going to be happy about my involvement in this.

"At?" he prompted.

I sighed. The question was probably inevitable. "Howard Academy." I pointed north. Up the hill.

Prudhoe nodded. He knew where it was.

The other two officers emerged from the building. Prudhoe went to join them, and they all conferred for several minutes. Faith and I hung around some more. Nobody was paying any attention to us now. I wondered if that meant we could leave. I was thinking about doing just that when I heard someone say my name.

"Ms. Travis?" It was the other officer who'd arrived in the second car. He was older and heavier than Prudhoe, and looked even less friendly. "I'm Officer Hurst. I'd like to ask you some questions about what happened here."

I shrugged. "I don't know what happened. I was inside the store for probably less than two minutes before Faith and I came back outside and called nine-one-one."

"Faith?" he asked.

She looked up at us and I gave her a pat.

Hurst frowned and moved on. "What was the nature of your business here?"

Considering that the place was a pet supply store and I was standing outside it with a dog on a leash, the question felt superfluous. At least to me. But Hurst looked like the kind of guy who wanted to dot all his *I*'s and cross all his *T*'s.

"I wanted to talk to Mr. Willet." I'd been interviewed by the police before. So I was well aware that that best answers were the shortest ones. Elaborating only seemed to raise more questions.

"About what?"

"My school is holding a fundraiser." I gestured toward the poster on the front window. "Along with many other businesses in town, Willet's Pet Supplies is participating. Which means that a number of our students have probably been in his store over the past week. I was told that he'd called the school last night to lodge a complaint. So I came here this morning to follow up."

Officer Hurst had been jotting down some notes. He looked up. "What was the complaint about?"

"I don't know. Mr. Willet didn't say in his message, and I never had a chance to talk to him."

"You're telling me he was dead when you got here?"

"Yes." Abruptly I swallowed a strangled breath. "I mean, I assume so. I only saw him from the hallway. I didn't . . . um . . . touch him."

Hurst shook his head slightly. I took that to mean that there hadn't been anything else I could have done. *Thank God.*

Two more official-looking vehicles arrived on the scene. One was the medical examiner's van. It pulled off the road and into the small lot, blocking most of the cars that were parked there. The other was a plain dark sedan. Its driver took his time about getting out.

"Officer Folger was first here on the scene," Officer Hurst continued. "You told him to be sure not to open the storeroom door. Why did you do that?"

"Because when I was inside, I could hear there was a dog in the room. Mr. Willet owns a Chow named Cider, who is often here at the store with him."

"Cider like the drink?"

"And his color," I added, which probably didn't help since Hurst hadn't yet seen the Chow. "He's a strong dog, and very attached to his owner. Cider sounded upset. I was afraid he'd get loose and something unfortunate might happen."

"I guess that means we'd better notify Animal Control."

I glanced at my watch. Kevin's kindergarten class was dismissed at one. Usually I picked him up outside his classroom, and he and I went home together. Now there was no telling how much longer I'd be held up. It was beginning to look as though I should make an alternate arrangement for him too.

Sam's work schedule had him tied up for most of the day. But with luck, Alice Brickman might be available. Alice and I had been best friends since we'd met at a neighborhood play group when Davey and her son, Joey, were toddlers. At the time, we'd lived right down the street from each other.

Alice and I were both well versed in the hectic demands of motherhood. We'd been covering for each other for years. When Alice's husband, Joe, made partner at his Greenwich law firm, she had quit her job to become a full-time mom. I hoped she might be available to step in.

"Just a few more questions," Officer Hurst said.

"Of course." Faith had been sitting patiently beside me. She must have intuited the sigh I'd smothered because she slowly walked her front feet outward, then lowered her body until she was lying down on the sidewalk. "Good girl," I murmured.

"You've said that you were inside the building this morning?" Hurst asked.

"Yes."

"But not inside Mr. Willet's office."

"No, just in the hallway." I was sure we'd covered that earlier.

"How did you know that the man you saw inside the office was Gregory Willet?"

"I'm not sure." I thought back. "I guess I just assumed it was him."

"Even though you only saw him from behind?" Hurst sounded skeptical. "How well did you know Mr. Willet?"

I frowned at the inference. "Aside from having shopped in his store, not at all."

"And yet you also know his dog's name and are familiar with the dog's temperament." He stated the facts in a flat tone, as if he seemed to think they were proof that I was lying to him.

So far, I'd cooperated. But now my patience was waning. "As I said a minute ago, Mr. Willet often had Cider in the store with him. He called the dog by name. And anyone who knows anything about Chows is aware that they can be aloof with strangers while being very loyal to their owners."

"Chows," Hurst muttered, again in disbelief.

"Are we finished?" I asked. There wasn't much point in my remaining there if he wasn't going to believe my answers to his questions.

"Let's just run through your statement one more time. You arrived and entered the store. You walked to the back, where you saw Mr. Willet slumped over his desk. At that point, you immediately exited the store."

"That sounds right."

"So you're saying we won't find your fingerprints inside Mr. Willet's office?"

I'd looked down at Faith, about to ask her to stand up so we could leave. But now I froze. My gaze slowly lifted. I stared at Officer Hurst.

"Excuse me?" This time I was the one who sounded disbelieving. "Am I a suspect?"

"Just answer the question, please, Ms. Travis."

Before I could reply, I became aware of a movement behind me. I turned and saw that the door to the dark sedan was now open. The car's occupant had gotten out and was heading our way.

Detective Raymond Young was a middle-aged Black man with a rangy body and close-cropped hair. A perceptive man, he was also smart enough to keep an open mind. Now he was coming toward us like a man on a mission. This wouldn't be the first time he and I had crossed paths in the course of a murder investigation.

Detective Young flashed me a quick look. Then his gaze went to Officer Hurst. "I'll take it from here."

"I'm in the middle of an interview," the officer protested. "You need to be aware that Ms. Travis has provided several contradictory answers—"

"Ms. Travis and I are well acquainted," Young told him. "You may leave the remainder of the interview in my hands. I'm sure I'll be able to ascertain the facts of the situation to your satisfaction."

Hurst looked doubtful. Then resigned. He spun on his heel and left.

"Thank you," I said when he was gone.

"Don't thank me yet," Detective Young replied. "I hear you've come across another dead body."

"I'm afraid so." Truthfully, I hadn't found that many. But each time it happened, the accompanying shock was deep and visceral. "I'll tell you what I know. But first, can you give me a minute to make a phone call?"

His brow lifted. "Russell Hanover?" The headmaster and the detective had also met before.

"Heaven forbid," I said. "No, this is about child care."

"Ahh. Of course." He stepped back while I made the call.

Fortunately, Alice answered right away. Even better, she was able to head to Howard Academy as soon as we got off the phone. I reminded her that Kevin's teacher's name was Jill Wheeler. Alice was already on my approved pickup list in the office, so that wouldn't be a problem. I thanked her profusely and turned back to the detective.

While I was talking to Alice, he and Faith had been having a moment. Young had stooped down in front of the Poodle and was stroking both sides of her body with his hands. Faith, who'd been mostly ignored for the previous half hour, was now wriggling with delight.

"Did you get everything squared away?" he asked, rising to his feet.

"Yes, thank you. Now what do you need to know?"

"Start at the beginning," Detective Young said. "And tell me everything."

So I did. Without saying a word, he managed to elicit more information from me in ten minutes than Officer Hurst's questions had in twice that amount of time. The difference was, I knew Detective Young wasn't suspicious of either my story or my motives. Also, based on our past experiences, I trusted him to do the right thing with any information I might relay.

At the end of my recitation, I circled back to something I'd been wondering about while I'd waited for the police to arrive. "What happened in there didn't look like a robbery," I said.

The detective glanced around briefly, then nodded. "As far as we've been able to tell, you're correct. Nothing else in the store appears to be have been disturbed, including the cash register and a small safe in the office."

"So that means Mr. Willet was personally targeted by whoever attacked him?" The situation was already bad enough. But somehow, that made it seem even worse.

Detective Young didn't answer my question, but that was all right. I'd mostly been thinking aloud anyway. I changed the subject. My next concern was for Mr. Willet's Chow.

"What will happen to Cider?" I asked.

"Animal Control will pick him up and hold him until Mr. Willet's next of kin can be notified. Hopefully, that person will then take custody of the dog. You don't need to worry about him. The AC guys know how to handle tough animals."

He must have been listening to what I'd said earlier.

"Cider isn't a bad dog," I assured him. "And despite all the noise he's making in there, he's not ferocious either. He's just upset about everything that happened. Whatever took place between Mr. Willet and the person who killed him, Cider probably heard all of it."

Detective Young looked shocked. Clearly, that hadn't occurred to him. "Are you telling me that dog in there is a witness?"

"I guess I am," I said.

Chapter
Five

Ten minutes later, Faith and I trudged back up the hill to Howard Academy. Well, I trudged. Faith was full of energy. She'd been doing nothing but waiting patiently for the past hour, so she was happy for the chance to run around.

My normal day at Howard Academy ended at one o'clock, and it was past that time now. I really wanted to take the coward's way out—go straight to the parking lot, pick up my car, and leave. But that wouldn't be fair to Harriet. I'd promised her an explanation. It was time to go in and face the music.

When I reached the mansion, however, I saw that Harriet was out front. She was sitting on the weathered stone steps that led to the entrance, munching on an apple, and trying to look as though this kind of bohemian behavior was an everyday occurrence on her part.

Which it most assuredly was not.

"Are you waiting for me?" I asked.

Harriet stood up and brushed off the back of her woolen skirt. She still hadn't met my eye. "I made one simple request," she grumbled under her breath. "Find out why Mr. Willet is unhappy and make him happy again. Is that too much to ask?"

"No," I said in a small voice as Faith came running up to stand beside me. She had a tennis ball in her mouth. She must have found it in the bushes.

"I didn't think so either." Harried sighed. "Now that the leaves are falling from the trees, you can actually see Putnam Avenue from here, if you know where to look. Were you aware of that?"

I nodded slowly.

"After I heard the first siren, I started looking. Imagine my surprise when I saw where the police cars were heading." She didn't sound surprised at all. "So, how bad is it?"

"Pretty bad," I said. "Mr. Willet is dead."

Even though she'd known bad news was coming, Harriet still winced. "Please tell me he died of natural causes. Maybe a heart attack or some genetic afflic- tion that can't possibly be blamed on his store's in- volvement in our fundraiser."

"No, sorry." I hated being the bearer of even more bad news. "He was stabbed in the back. It must have happened shortly before I arrived. I was the one who found him."

"Of course you were." Now Harriet sounded resigned. "Whenever something goes wrong, you always seem to be right in the middle of it."

"Sorry?" Another apology seemed called for, even though it wasn't really my fault.

"You're going to get involved, aren't you?"

"Actually I hadn't thought that far ahead."

The sight of Mr. Willet's body was still depressingly fresh in my mind. I hadn't been able to move past that image to consider anything else.

"Then let me answer that question for you," Harriet said.

She marched over to stand in front of me, close enough that we were almost nose to nose. Her hand ruffled gently through Faith's topknot, but the look she directed at me was made of steel. "Yes, you are going to get involved. First, because I know you, Melanie. When bad things happen, that's what you do."

I closed my eyes briefly. When I opened them again, Harriet was still there. Of course she was. She hadn't yet finished making her point.

"And second," she continued, "because we—by which I mean Howard Academy—need you to quickly and quietly come up with answers that direct attention away from our school. The press, the parents, and anyone else who might be interested, must be convinced that Mr. Willet's association with our fundraiser was merely an unfortunate coincidence. That a member of our faculty found his body was just bad luck. That in no way was this institution associated with what happened."

Harriet wasn't Russell Hanover's second-in-command for nothing. Like our headmaster, she believed unequivocally in Howard Academy's academic and social missions. She'd devoted her life to the school's advancement and prosperity. And she wasn't about to let some pip-squeak like me come along and screw it all up.

Harriet and I might be friends, but her first loyalty was to the school. She and Mr. Hanover would do anything in their power to protect the institution and its reputation. No matter who else paid the cost.

"Am I making myself clear?" she asked.

"Yes." Now that I'd been thoroughly lectured, I had nothing left to add.

"Good." Harriet stepped back. "Don't worry about Mr. Hanover. I'll keep everything copacetic there. That man's a worrier. And he has a board meeting coming up next week. Right now, the fewer outside distractions he has to deal with, the better."

I nodded gratefully. If Harriet was willing to run interference for me with the Big Guy, that would definitely make my life easier. On the other hand, she'd also just assigned me a task that I might or might not be able to perform to her exacting specifications. I wasn't sure whether I'd won or lost in the exchange.

"You know the police will be investigating Mr. Willet's murder," I pointed out.

"Of course."

"I can't control what they do or what they might say to the media."

Harriet reached out and placed a hand on my shoulder. Her features softened. She smiled at me in a grandmotherly way. "I'm sure you'll figure something out, dear. You always do."

I'd have felt better about her vote of confidence if I actually believed it.

Alice Brickman and her family lived in Stamford, in a subdivision built in the middle of the previous century. Each street had a row of clapboard cottages with small backyards. The neighborhood was quiet and friendly. Children played on the sidewalks, and residents greeted each other by name. It was a wonderful place to raise a family.

Before Sam and I got married and merged our households, Alice and I had lived just a few doors down from each other. Though I'd moved to North Stamford, she and I remained close and still spoke often.

Driving down the neighborhood's narrow streets to the Brickmans' house felt like revisiting my past.

When I hopped Faith out of the car, she knew where I was going and immediately ran on ahead. Alice was expecting me—she had my child, after all—so her front door was open. Only the glass storm door was closed. I took that as an invitation to let myself in.

As I reached for the latch, Alice's Golden Retriever, Berkley, began to bark. He liked to think he was a watchdog. While his size might have been intimidating, the entire neighborhood knew he was a big cream puff. Like their owners, Berkley and Faith had been friends for years. Both dogs' tails were sweeping back and forth as they pressed their noses to the glass pane between them.

"Melanie, is that you?" Alice called from the back of the house.

"You'd better hope so," I said with a laugh. "Come and help with the door. I have my hands full."

A moment later, Alice appeared in the small entryway. She was dressed in a cream-colored flannel shirt, worn untucked over a pair of mom jeans. A profusion of strawberry blond curls formed a halo around her face. Alice was five years older than me, a gap that had once felt large but now seemed almost infinitesimal.

"Oh goodie!" she cried happily, as she pushed the storm door open. "Is that what I think it is?"

"Pumpkin spice lattes," I said. "One for each of us. Although Kevin's is mostly made of whipped cream. After you were kind enough to pick him up from school, I could hardly arrive empty-handed."

"Don't be silly," Alice scoffed as she took the cardboard container that held the three covered cups out of my hands. "You'd have done the same for me."

"And have," I pointed out, and we smiled together.

Alice led the way back to the kitchen. The dogs followed in our wake.

Kevin was seated at a wooden table pushed up against a side wall. He had a pad of plain white drawing paper and a box of crayons in front of him. There was a pile of fresh leaves in the center of the table. My child was so absorbed in what he was doing that he barely bothered to look up when we entered the room.

"Hi, Mom," I said, nudging the back of his chair.

"Hi, Mom," he repeated dutifully, still intent on his project.

Alice smirked. Not because her children had better manners than mine, but because, being older, they were currently still in school and therefore unable to demonstrate their utter disregard for the parent who'd loved and nurtured them since birth.

"That looks like fun," I said to Kevin.

"I'm doing leaf rubbings," he told me. "Mrs. Brickman and I collected the leaves from her yard. She said I can make as many as I want."

I leaned over and took a look. "How many have you done so far?"

"At least a dozen," Alice replied. "Right, Kev?"

"Right," he agreed, then went back to work. Faith lay down on one side of his chair. Berkley did the same on the other side.

Alice handed out the three drinks, then set the container aside on a counter. "Kevin can entertain himself here for at least another half hour," she said to me. "Why don't we go into the living room and chat?"

"Good idea."

The cozy living room was in the front of the house on the other side of the hall. With two teenagers in residence, its furniture had clearly been chosen with practicality in mind. Alice plopped down in a deep-cushioned armchair. I walked around a coffee table and sat down across from her on a corduroy-covered couch.

"Kevin's having a great time," I said. "Thank you for not just sticking him in front of a TV, especially since this was such short notice."

"As if." She snorted. "I'm an old hand at this mothering thing. I have project ideas for every day of the week."

"Your diligence is noted. And much appreciated."

Alice waved away the compliment. She snapped the plastic top off the latte cup, then closed her eyes and inhaled deeply. "Oh, that's perfection. Is it any wonder fall is my favorite season of the year?"

I laughed. "I thought it was because that's when the kids go back to school."

"That, too. And speaking of school . . ." She glanced back in the direction of the kitchen. As long as we kept our voices down, Kevin wouldn't be able to hear what we were saying. "What happened earlier?"

"You probably don't want to know."

"Of course I do. The only reason I have any excitement in my life at all is because I live vicariously through you. What kind of trouble did you get yourself into this time?"

"I told you about the Howard Academy fundraiser, right?"

"Right. Thanks for Giving." Alice made a face. "A third-grader could have come up with that slogan."

"It was Mr. Hanover's idea. Since he's the school's headmaster, we all automatically loved it."

"Noted. Continue."

"There's a treasure hunt—"

"Also not news," Alice said. "You can move this along. And should. Otherwise we'll be here until dinner."

"The owner of one of the participating stores had a complaint about the contest." I held up a hand to forestall the inevitable question. "Don't ask me what it was about, because I don't know. I was sent downtown to Willet's Pet Supplies this morning to find out."

Alice had lifted the cup to her lips to take another sip. Instead, her hand stilled. Her eyes widened fractionally.

"What?" I asked.

"It's nothing."

"You're thinking something. And if it's enough to make you stop drinking a pumpkin spice latte, it must be important."

Alice shook her head. She took a large swallow of her drink as if to indicate that she wasn't perturbed at all. "Pet supplies. I just remembered I need to buy more dog food for Berkley."

I didn't believe that for a minute. But Alice clearly wanted me to change the subject. And since I owed her, I obliged.

"When I arrived at the store, the owner, Gregory Willet, was indisposed."

"What does that mean?" she asked. "How was he indisposed?"

"Actually, he was deceased."

"Like dead?" she squeaked.

"Very much like dead," I confirmed. "I was trying not to offend your delicate sensibilities."

"Oh please. I've changed approximately a million diapers in my life. I don't have any delicate sensibilities left. How dead was he?"

I paused to take a sip of my latte and lick the foam off my lip, then said, "I wasn't aware that was a quantifiable condition."

"No, I mean like did it happen recently . . . or maybe last week, but nobody noticed until now?"

"The former."

"And you were the one who found him?" Alice stood up and set her cup down on the table. Then she came around to sit beside me. She wrapped her arms around my shoulders and held on tight. "You poor thing. That must have been terrible."

"It was. There was a lot of blood."

Abruptly she drew back. "Okay, no gory details. Apparently I do have one or two functioning sensibilities left."

"Got it," I said. "Slightly new topic then. Harriet wants me to find out what happened so the school won't be implicated in any way."

"Harriet, the headmaster's assistant?" Alice asked.

"Yes."

"The woman who's capable of making grown men quake in their boots?"

"The very one."

"Then you probably ought to do what she tells you."

"That's what I thought," I said.

Alice looked at me and frowned. "You were going to do that anyway, weren't you?"

I shrugged like I wasn't sure. That was a lie. It wasn't even a good one.

Alice was right, and we both knew it.

Chapter
Six

Tuesday afternoon after school, I dropped Kevin and Faith off at home, then returned to Greenwich. Since Sam was self-employed, he was able to set his own schedule. On busy days, I wasn't above taking advantage of that. Once I'd delegated responsibility for our child and dogs to him, I was free to return to Mr. Willet's store.

Nightmares had kept me up for most of the previous night. I'd awakened in a cold sweat, imagining that with all the commotion surrounding Mr. Willet's death, Cider had somehow been forgotten. I'd pictured the poor Chow, stuck inside the storeroom, and still waiting for someone to rescue him. That felt like a good excuse to pay another visit to the pet supply store.

I'd called earlier to check that the store was open today. Now when I arrived, I saw that not only was the place open, there were quite a few customers inside. Apparently murder was good for business.

I walked through the door and strode down the nearest aisle toward the back of the building. Bags of kibble on the shelves around me filled the air with a familiar aroma. A king-size box of peanut butter biscuits caught my eye and I paused briefly, then gave myself a mental shake. I wasn't here to shop.

There was a checkout counter on one side of the store. The day before, that area had been empty. Now a line had formed there. Several people had their arms full. They were buying everything from designer dog leashes to kitty litter.

A man in his twenties with short, dark hair and an intent expression on his face was behind the counter. I watched as he quickly rang up and bagged several purchases. He never even glanced up from what he was doing.

No one else was paying any attention to me either. It was a good thing I'd left Faith at home. When we went places together, people often took note of my "giant" Poodle. Now, by myself, I was just another customer.

I sidled over to the short hallway that led to Mr. Willet's office and the storeroom across from it. The office door was closed, and it had been sealed with yellow crime scene tape. That was to be expected.

The storeroom door was also shut. At least it didn't have any tape on it. I stood for a moment and listened. I couldn't hear any sounds coming from within.

"Sorry, this area is off limits," a voice said from behind me.

I turned and saw that the salesclerk had finished dealing with the line of people and emerged from behind the counter. He was several inches taller than me and had striking hazel-green eyes. He didn't look pleased.

So much for not being noticed.

"Can I help you find something?" Clearly he was eager to steer me away from the back of the store. "Dog or cat?" When I didn't reply right away, he offered more options. "Hamster? Snake? Rabbit?"

I smiled in spite of myself. "Dogs. Lots of them. But that's actually not why I'm here."

Abruptly his expression hardened. "If you're a reporter, I have nothing to say, and I'm going to have to ask you to leave."

"I'm not a reporter," I said quickly. "I was here . . . yesterday. I'm the person who . . ." I gestured toward the sealed office door.

His gaze slid to the door, then back to me. He looked as though he still didn't understand.

"I found Mr. Willet." My voice was scarcely louder than a whisper. "I'm the person who called the police."

He stared at me for a second, his eyes widening. "I'm so sorry. I had no idea. That must have been an awful shock."

I nodded, and he lifted his head to look around the store. "Let me just take care of these customers, then I'll put the closed sign on the door for a few minutes. That is . . . if you'd like to talk?"

"I would. Thank you."

"There's a bench in the book section. You can wait there if you want, and I'll be over shortly."

The pet care books were in a small alcove with a high window that provided extra light. A whole wall was devoted to showcasing dozens of colorful titles. The middle shelf held the Book of the Week: *Tortoises Make Great Pets*. A wooden bench, painted bright blue and placed nearby, invited shoppers to sit and browse through the selections. Ten minutes later, I was still checking out the dog books when the clerk reappeared.

"Trevor Pine," he said, holding out his hand.

"Melanie Travis," I replied. "Thank you for taking the time to talk to me."

"We probably don't have long," he said. "I've never seen the store this busy before. Not even around the holidays. We were closed yesterday afternoon, but as soon as I opened this morning, people started coming in to gawk. Then most of them end up buying something because they feel guilty. I know there's supposed to be no such thing as bad publicity, but this seems insane to me."

"I know," I said. "I'm baffled too. I have no idea why a tragic occurrence seems to draw people in."

"If you don't mind my asking . . ." Trevor paused, waiting until I nodded. "What brought you back here? After what you experienced yesterday, I wouldn't blame you if you never wanted to come near this place again."

"It was Cider," I said. "I kept having nightmares about him last night."

"The dog?" Trevor sounded surprised. Under the circumstances, I could understand why.

"When I got here yesterday, Cider was locked in the storeroom. But he must have known something was wrong because he kept throwing himself against the door. Faith and I both heard him. It was really disturbing."

"Faith?"

"She's my Standard Poodle."

"Ahh, I guess that explains why you were here."

"Actually, no. I came because I needed to talk to Mr. Willet. I'm a teacher at Howard Academy, and he'd agreed to take part in our fundraiser."

"Sure," Trevor agreed. "He told me all about it. I'm the one who hung up your poster."

"I appreciate that. But on Sunday, the school got a message that Mr. Willet wanted to make a complaint.

He didn't specify what it was. I don't suppose you know anything about it?"

Trevor shook his head. "Not a thing. This is the first I'm hearing of it. I can't imagine Mr. Willet had a gripe about any of the kids. We've had a steady stream of them coming in since last week. For the most part, they've all been polite and well-mannered."

"That's nice to hear."

"Not only that, but I'm getting a kick out of hiding those pumpkin spice tokens of yours," he continued. "I made the first batch too easy to find—and learned my lesson when they all got scooped up right away. Now I'm trying to make the search more of a challenge."

"Good idea," I said with a smile. "Let me know when you need to restock. I'll be happy to stop by and drop off some more."

"I will. But getting back to that complaint you mentioned. Usually I work here part-time, just in the afternoons. So it's possible that something happened when I wasn't around. Do you think whatever it was could be connected to Mr. Willet's death?"

"I hope not," I replied fervently. "Howard Academy would hate to have its name mentioned in connection with a crime. Best case for the school would be if the police decide to look in every other direction first."

Trevor glanced toward the door. No one was waiting to come in. "We've still got a minute or two before I need to open up again. Since you were worried about Cider, do you want to go say hello to him?"

"He's here?" I hadn't expected that.

"Sure." Trevor gestured toward the storeroom. "He's still a bit agitated today, so I put him in a crate. Poor guy, with everything that happened, it's not his fault. But I still feel better if he's confined. I've been popping in to check on him every half hour or so."

We walked to the back of the store together. "The police said they were going to have Animal Control pick him up, then hold him until they could figure out where he was supposed to go."

"Yeah, they told me the same thing yesterday when I arrived for my shift. Apparently someone had warned them not to let him out of the storeroom." Trevor looked over at me. "Was that you?"

I nodded. "I could hear how upset he was, and I didn't want anything stupid to happen."

"Thank you for that." Trevor reached down and opened the door. "You probably saved Cider a whole lot of unnecessary grief. He and I have been buddies for a while. He was pretty frantic by the time I arrived, but I was able to get him calmed down and gave him some water. Cider wasn't happy about all the strangers milling around, so I took him outside and put him in my car."

The light was on in the storeroom, and the temperature was comfortably warm. Cider was lying down in a wire crate that was big enough to give him plenty of room to move and turn around. He hopped to his feet as soon as he saw us.

Cider was a red Chow, with a thick coat that formed a wide ruff around his neck. His head was large, with dark, deep-set eyes. Medium in size, he had a broad chest and a muscular body. His tail flipped up over his back.

Cider stared at me disdainfully. Then his gaze went to Trevor and he opened his mouth in a doggy grin that showed off his blue-black tongue.

"Hey there, big boy," Trevor crooned. "Want to come out and play?"

Cider woofed softly in reply. I stood to one side as Trevor opened the crate. Cider came bounding out into his arms and nearly knocked him over. Seconds later, it was my turn to be greeted. I held out a hand for the dog to smell. That earned me a look of dignified disregard.

"I feel like I'm meeting the king," I said with a laugh.

"Cider would probably agree with you." Trevor laughed too. "He doesn't lack for confidence. And since you're new, he'll expect you to earn his regard. But don't worry, he'll warm up to you soon enough."

"What will happen to him long-term?" I asked.

"I don't know," Trevor said unhappily. "And unfortunately, it's not up to me. For now he's staying at my place. The detective was okay with that as long as they knew where he was. Last night Cider slept on my bed and tried to hog all the pillows."

"Yeah, I can see that." I glanced at the Chow, who was now sniffing his way around the room. "What about the store? Will it close now that Mr. Willet's gone? You said this was only a part-time job for you. Is there someone else available to take over?"

"Actually, someone is taking over. And you're looking at him." I turned back to Trevor, and he nodded. "Overnight, I found myself promoted from assistant to store manager. This gig just became my full-time job. Based on that, I'm assuming the store will stay in business for a while, at least until things get sorted out."

"I thought this was Mr. Willet's store," I said, surprised. "Who's making the decisions now?"

"Julia Geist is the one who called me." When I looked at him blankly, he clarified. "Mr. Willet's ex-wife. It turns out she's part owner of this place."

"Does that give her the authority to hire staff?" I wondered.

"Beats me." Trevor shrugged. "All I know is that she wants the store open and earning income. When I told her I was available to take on more hours, she jumped at the chance. She even gave me a raise."

Maybe that was hardship pay, I mused. Plenty of people would think twice about continuing to work in a store where a murder had recently taken place.

"I guess you must have known Mr. Willet pretty well," I said.

"I suppose so. I've worked here for more than a year."

"So his death must have come as a shock to you too."

"Of course it did." Trevor went to retrieve Cider. He placed his hands on either side of the Chow's body to guide him back into his crate. "No one expects to be in a situation like this in real life."

Unfortunately the same couldn't be said for me. This was far from the first time I'd been involved in something similar. I wasn't about to confess that to Trevor, however.

I waited until he'd fastened the latch and straightened to face me, then said, "You must have given it some thought. Why do you think someone would have wanted to harm Mr. Willet?"

Trevor opened his mouth. Then closed it again. He rubbed a hand over his chin as he considered the idea. He didn't appear to like it much.

"I watch plenty of movies," he said finally. "I guess the guilty party almost always seems to be the ex, doesn't it?"

Chapter
Seven

Julia Geist wasn't hard to locate. As soon as I did an online search for her name, more than a dozen notices popped up.

She was involved in a number of educational and environmental causes, both around town and elsewhere. Not only that, she also appeared to document much of her life, and her schedule, on social media. That was how I learned that she'd be at the Greenwich Library that afternoon, helping out with a children's literacy program.

For people who love books or Greenwich history, the library is a wondrous place. Set on a busy corner just west of downtown, the imposing building has large windows, stacks of resources, and a convenient parking lot out back. I arrived just as the program was due to end, and parked in a spot from which I could see the door.

Ten minutes later, Julia Geist emerged from the

building. She was a petite woman of around fifty, dressed in a navy blue pantsuit with an Hermès scarf tied around her neck. Her hair and makeup were impeccable. She skipped down the steps in heels that were higher than any I'd ever worn in my life.

By the time she reached the sidewalk, I was there waiting for her. "Excuse me," I said. "Julia Geist?"

She paused and turned. "Yes. Can I help you?"

"My name is Melanie Travis. I'm hoping I can have a few minutes of your time to talk about Gregory Willet?"

She took a moment to look me over. I was wearing a wool peacoat over comfy corduroy pants and had chunky-heeled boots on my feet. I was certainly presentable but, by her standards, maybe a bit scruffy.

"You don't look like a reporter," she said.

"I'm not. I'm a teacher at Howard Academy." I hoped that might add to my credibility. The public Julia was in favor of a great education for all children. Free lunches too, for that matter.

Her brow rose. "Shouldn't you be in school?"

"I'm the special needs tutor. And a mom," I told her. "I work part-time from eight-thirty to one."

"Good for you," she said briskly. "I'm not sure why you're here, though. Gregory is my ex-husband. I have nothing to say about him that would be of interest."

"I'd be happy to explain. Do you have time for a cup of coffee?"

She checked her watch before replying. I suspected she was stalling for time while deciding whether or not to grant me an interview. Then her eyes lifted. "I can spare ten minutes," she said. "And I drink tea."

Luckily, there was a coffee shop right across the street. Even better, it wasn't crowded. So when we were settled in our seats with our drinks in front of us, I hadn't used up much of my allotted time.

I could smell her drink from across the table. "I didn't know there was such a thing as pumpkin spice tea," I said.

"Pumpkin spice and chai spices are very similar," Julia told me. "This time of year, shops serve nearly the same tea and call it pumpkin spice for marketing purposes."

That made me laugh. I'd had no idea. "Can you blame them?"

"Not at all." Julia picked up her cup. "You wanted to talk to me about Gregory?"

So much for small talk. I could be direct, too, if that was what she wanted.

"How did you learn about your ex-husband's death?" I asked.

"A friend called me," she said blandly.

The reply reminded me that Julia was the kind of person who would have connections all over town.

As it was probably meant to. "Were you surprised by the news?"

"Possibly less than I should have been." She paused, then frowned. "I'm sorry. That sounded callous, which wasn't my intent. My marriage with Gregory had a perfectly satisfactory beginning, followed by several years that can only be labeled as contentious, before coming to an inevitable end. We've been divorced for quite a while. Frankly, I don't waste much time thinking about Gregory at all anymore."

She peered at me across the table. "Why is this any of your business?"

Julia seemed like she would appreciate honesty, so I didn't beat around the bush. "My school is running a fundraiser and Mr. Willet's store was involved. Due to that circumstance, I inadvertently became the person who discovered his body yesterday."

She'd been sipping her tea. Now she gasped, then choked slightly.

"Sorry," I said as she put her cup down. "Too blunt?"

"Not at all. Please continue."

"As you may know, Howard Academy has a sterling reputation."

"Sterling," Julia repeated with a nod to confirm that we were in agreement about that.

"And of course, an association with an unexplained death—"

"Murder," Julia corrected me. "Yes, I can see how that might upset the trustees, not to mention potential donors. Where do you fit in?"

"As it happens, I've solved a few murder mysteries in the past."

A smiled played around Julia's lips. "That seems unlikely."

I shrugged and took a swallow of my coffee—black with just a touch of cream. There wasn't much I could do to convince her to believe me.

"You're not joking," she said.

"No."

"And you think I might have wanted to kill my ex-husband?" Her voice lifted slightly. "Is that why we're here?"

"It seemed like a question worth asking," I pointed out.

"Because he and I are divorced?"

"Because you probably know him better than most people." I paused, then added, "And perhaps because of those contentious years."

Julia sat back in her seat. "You're no dummy." She sounded pleased by that discovery.

"No, I'm not."

"Good. The children who will grow up to lead the world tomorrow should have smart teachers today. Go ahead, ask me what you want to know. If it's not too personal, I'll answer. This remains strictly between you and me, you understand."

"I do. Why did you and Mr. Willet—Gregory—get divorced?"

"He cheated on me," Julia replied. "More than once. It started when I was pregnant with our daughter, Lucia, then continued off and on for several years after she was born. Gregory wanted children in theory. Not so much in practice."

I nodded and briefly thought back to my first husband. The refrain was familiar. He was an ex now, too. Obviously.

"Children are messy," she was saying. "Sometime they cry and throw tantrums. Then they get bigger and talk back. It turned out that Gregory preferred dogs. Chow Chows, of all things. Big, hairy beasts." She shuddered.

"Like Cider," I said. "The dog who was with him at the store."

"If you say so." That topic wasn't of much interest to her.

"I understand that you're part owner of his store."

"*His* store." Julia sniffed indelicately. "I'm the one who provided the seed money to open that business. We were married then, of course. Even so, I made him sign a contract. I was no dummy either."

Julia and I smiled together.

"What were the terms of the contract?"

"He owned fifty-one percent of the business, I own forty-nine. *Men.*" She shook her head. "They always need to feel as though they're the ones in charge. But I didn't care about that. It wasn't as though I wanted to have the right to make decisions about *pet supplies.*"

I almost smiled again, but caught myself just in time.

"For the first three years, profits—if there were any—would be rolled back in, to grow and support the business. After that, half of all profits made would come to me, off the top, until such time as my loan was paid off. And yes, before you ask, it was also written into the document that upon either of our deaths, ownership of the store would revert to the surviving partner."

"Is Willet's Pet Supplies profitable?" I asked curiously. I knew the store sat on a piece of prime Greenwich real estate. That alone seemed to indicate that it must be making money.

"Yes. It has been almost from the beginning. For all his faults, Gregory knew how to attract customers and keep them happy."

"And has he paid back the money you loaned him?"

"No." Julia frowned again. "Less than half. Once we were divorced, the payments Gregory made became spotty, then eventually ceased all together. When I called him on it, he told me the store was going through a rough patch. He complained about higher costs and lower revenues. Taxes were going up, the building needed maintenance, things like that."

"Did you believe him?" I asked.

Julia still didn't look happy. Her fingers were playing with a packet of sweetener on the table. "No, I didn't. He and I had a fight about it. A rather large one. He offered to show me the books, as though he thought that would placate me. By that time, I wouldn't have trusted him not to be keeping two sets."

"You had a contract," I pointed out. "You could have sued him."

"Yes, I could have," she agreed. "But two things stopped me. For one, he's Lucia's father. Not that he's ever been the best parent, but at least he took a stab at being part of her life."

"How old is your daughter now?" I asked. "Is he still involved?"

"Less so than when she was younger. Lucia's an adult, she turned twenty-three last month." Julia sounded like a proud mother. "She graduated from college in the spring, traveled in Europe over the summer, and now she's living at home with me while she looks for a job."

I nodded. "What's the other reason?"

"This one should be obvious. The whole point of the divorce was I wanted to get Gregory *out* of my life. And a lawsuit would have given him a reason to worm his way back in." She sighed. "Not that he's seemed to need a reason recently."

I was pretty sure my ten minutes were just about up. I tipped back my head and finished the last of my coffee. "What do you mean by that?"

"Just that he'd been hanging around more than usual. Showing up at the house and acting like he somehow thought he was still part of the family. As if I would ever allow that to happen. He used the excuse that Lucia had been away, and now that she was back, he wanted to visit her. For years, the man was an absentee father. Now, when it was far too late, he seemed to think he should have a say in how Lucia lives her life."

"That seems odd," I said.

"Not to me." Julia pushed back her chair and stood up. "If I had to guess, I'd say Gregory was probably having money problems. Whenever his funds ran low, he always came back to the source." Her lips twisted cynically. "Did I mention that I had to pay him alimony for ten years after the divorce?"

"No, you didn't."

We both picked up our cups and carried them over to the trash. "Believe me, it was worth it to get rid of him," she said.

As we left the coffee shop, I wondered how much it would have been worth to Julia to get rid of Gregory permanently. Not just financially, but mentally and emotionally, too. Maybe she'd just wanted to be done with the aggravation.

I knew how that felt. Though my ex and I were friendly now, my divorce from Davey's father had taken a similar toll at the time.

Both our cars were in the library parking lot across the street. We waited on the sidewalk for the traffic light to change. That gave me another minute or two. I wasn't about to waste them.

"Who might have hated your ex-husband enough to want to kill him?" I asked.

Julia glanced over. "You mean aside from me?"

"Sure." I wasn't about to rise to that bait.

"Perhaps Erik Poole. He was certainly angry enough."

"What's his connection to Gregory?"

"He lives next door. Poor guy. That dog you saw at the store? He's not Gregory's only Chow. My ex loves the breed. He takes in strays and rescues and fosters them until he can find them good homes. I can only imagine the chaos that causes. I haven't seen it for myself, but according to Lucia, he has as many as three or four in the house at a time. Untrained, unsocialized, hairy dogs with big teeth running loose all over the place."

Lots of dogs had big teeth, I thought. It didn't seem worth mentioning.

"Or around the neighborhood when he lets them out," she added.

"Gregory doesn't have a fenced yard?"

She spared me a glance. "What do you think?"

I guessed that was a *no*.

"Also Marshall Hamm." Julia almost seemed to be enjoying herself now. "He lives across the street. Same problem."

The light turned yellow, then red. As soon as the WALK sign came on, we both began to move.

"Can you give me Gregory's address?" I asked.

Julia took out her phone. "Let me have your number, and I'll text it to you. And do me a favor. If you talk to his neighbors, don't tell them I sent you."

We paused on the other side of the road and completed the transaction.

"Good luck," she said, as we went our separate ways in the parking lot.

"Thank you," I replied. "I suspect I'm going to need it."

Chapter
Eight

Gregory Willet's address was in Cos Cob, a town on the Connecticut coast between Greenwich—where I was then—and Stamford, where my family would be expecting me home at some later point. That felt like a sign, as if the Fates were telling me where to go next. And who was I to argue with destiny?

I found Mr. Willet's house easily enough. It was located in a pleasant residential neighborhood whose split-level houses looked like they dated from the 1970s. Homeowners maintained their properties with care. Most yards were meticulously landscaped. Lawns had been raked free of fallen leaves.

In comparison with the others on the road, there was nothing notable about Willet's house, except for its current air of solitude. There weren't any cars parked in the driveway, and the blinds in the front windows were lowered and shut. I wondered if that was meant to keep any Chows in residence from looking out at the street and barking at passersby.

With that thought came another. If Willet was currently fostering any dogs, I hoped someone had stepped in to take care of them in his absence. From what Julia had said, that person wasn't likely to have been his neighbor, Erik Poole. But I'd be sure to ask anyway.

Or I would have, if Erik Poole had been home. Considering that it was four o'clock on a weekday afternoon, maybe I hadn't thought this plan through as thoroughly as I should have. Now the Fates were reminding me of something they hadn't bothered to mention earlier. I had no idea of the man's age or occupation. It was likely that he was still at work. For all I knew, Willet's other neighbor, Marshall Hamm, might be unavailable as well.

I returned to my car and gazed across the street. The home opposite Willet's had bricks on its first story, then weathered shingles above. A row of neatly tended bushes accompanied a flagstone walk to the front door.

As I looked for a name on the mailbox, a curtain moved in a front window, as though someone had pulled it aside to take a peek out. Maybe this quiet street didn't get many visitors. Or maybe, after what had happened to Gregory Willet, his neighbors had become concerned about security. But at least it meant someone was home.

I had to knock twice before the door was opened by a man in his seventies who was built like a barrel. What little hair he had left was white, matching the stubble along his jawline. He was dressed in rumpled pants and a chunky sweater, with slippers on his feet. He looked disgruntled before I even had a chance to open my mouth.

"Whatever you're selling, I don't want any," he said.

"I'm not selling anything—"

"Good. Then go away." The door started to close.

"Mr. Hamm," I said quickly, lifting a hand to forestall that motion, "a mutual acquaintance recommended that I speak with you."

The door stilled. He peered out around it. "Mutual acquaintance?" he growled. "Who would that be?"

Darn it, I'd told Julia I wouldn't use her name. "I'm looking into your neighbor's murder," I said instead.

"What neighbor is that?"

As if he didn't know. A murder in Greenwich was news. The story had been all over the media.

"Gregory Willet."

"Are you some kind of detective?"

Some kind was about right. "Yes," I replied.

"You got an official ID?"

"Not on me," I admitted.

"Sounds fishy to me," he muttered. Then, to my surprise, he drew the door open again. "But I guess I wouldn't mind a little company. You might as well come inside before I let all the hot air out of my house. Heating bill's already sky high as it is." Mr. Hamm paused to look me up and down. "But you'd better behave yourself. You cause any trouble, I'm pretty sure I could take you."

"I'm pretty sure you could too," I said with a small smile.

"Lucky for you my soaps are done for the day," he told me as I followed him into a living room that was brightly lit and spotlessly neat. "You might as well sit down. Don't expect me to offer you any refreshments."

"No, sir," I said.

"And don't call me sir!"

Right. "How about Mr. Hamm?"

"That'll do," he grumbled.

I wasn't sure how long Mr. Hamm's goodwill might last. I figured I'd better get right down to business.

"I understand Mr. Willet's Chows have been causing problems here in your neighborhood," I said as we chose seats opposite each other.

"Chows," he repeated with a frown. "You mean those wild dogs of his?"

"Yes." Cider wasn't a wild dog, but I wasn't about to argue semantics.

"They're a menace to life and limb! Greg's supposed to keep those damn animals under control. That's the law."

"Yes," I agreed, hoping he'd keep talking.

"I may be an old man, but that doesn't mean I want to be stuck inside my house all day. Before I can even get my mail, I have to stand on the step and look both ways. Those damn dogs are sneaky. Turn your back and they could bowl you right over!"

"Maybe they're just being playful," I said.

"There's nothing playful about a man my age hitting the dirt in his own front yard," Mr. Hamm snapped. "I could break a hip."

He had a point.

"And what if one of them bit me? I could get rabies."

"Only if they were rabid," I said. "Which seems unlikely."

"I'll tell you what's unlikely." He lifted his hand and shook his finger at me. "A man choosing to harbor wild animals in a quiet neighborhood like this. Greg's dogs belong in a zoo."

The man had a way with hyperbole. I wondered if he was a writer.

"Did you ever talk to him about the problem?" I asked.

"Talk?" he huffed. "*Talk!* I complained until I was blue in the face. And where did it get me? Nowhere. All I got was a lecture about how many poor, homeless dogs there are in the world, and what a saint Greg was for being willing to rescue them."

"I take it you didn't agree about the sainthood aspect?"

Mr. Hamm stared at me, eyes narrowed, as if he was trying to decide whether I was making fun of him. "Don't you get fresh with me, young lady," he said. "I have a legitimate grievance."

"Yes, you did," I replied. "But not anymore."

"What?"

"Now that Mr. Willet is dead, his Chows will leave the neighborhood."

"Good riddance to the whole lot of them!" he snapped.

As soon as the words were out of his mouth, Mr. Hamm abruptly went still, then attempted to look as if he'd been struck by that realization for the very first time. Unfortunately for his purposes, the man wasn't as good an actor as he thought he was.

"I'd imagine that's what all that brouhaha was about last night," he said after a minute.

"What brouhaha?" I asked.

"Someone showed up across the street with a van.

Maybe around six o'clock. That's when I sit down to watch the news, but I saw lights on over there. Maybe they were loading up those animals and taking them away."

"Were you aware at that point that Gregory had been killed earlier in the day?"

Mr. Hamm dipped his head in a sharp nod.

"When you saw unusual activity taking place at his house, did it occur to you to call the police?"

"Not me," he replied. "I mind my own business."

The man had a twitching front curtain that said differently.

"So you think the Chows were removed from the house," I mused. It made sense. The police would have wanted to search Willet's place. They must have made the arrangements to have the dogs picked up.

"Could be. Leastways, I haven't heard them barking all day. Let me tell you, that's a big improvement around here."

"I'm sure it is," I agreed. "Aside from his Chows, was Mr. Willet a good neighbor?"

"What's that supposed to mean?" Mr. Hamm demanded. "Are you trying to trick me into speaking ill of the dead?"

It seemed to me we'd been doing that for the past several minutes. I didn't see any reason to stop now.

"I was just wondering how well the two of you got along otherwise."

"Just fine," he retorted. Any minute now he'd be offering to swear on a stack of Bibles that they were best friends.

"Had you and he lived across from each other for a long time?"

"Years. Probably close to twenty. Greg moved in here when his wife threw him out. He called this place his bachelor pad." Mr. Hamm cackled out a laugh. "That was wishful thinking on his part. Last ten years or so, the only thing going in and out of that house with any regularity were his dogs."

"Not his daughter?" I asked curiously.

"You mean Lucia?"

"Yes."

"Friendly little thing, that gal."

"She's all grown up now," I said. "She graduated from college this year."

"Time flies, doesn't it?" Mr. Hamm shook his head. "No, she was never around much. I can't remember the last time I saw her over there. It seems a shame when families break up like that."

"Maybe Mr. Willet was hard to live with."

"No, that wasn't it," he told me firmly. "His wife was the one who was the shrew. Greg told me all about it."

"There might be two sides to that story," I said.

He frowned. "You think?"

I nodded.

Mr. Hamm didn't look convinced.

*   *   *

I arrived home to find my house lit up like we were having a party.

Then I saw Aunt Peg's maroon minivan parked beside the garage. That explained things. As far as she was concerned, once she'd arrived, it *was* a party. I had to admit, though, things did liven up when Aunt Peg was around.

My family and I live in in a colonial-style house on two acres of land, far from the bustling center of Stamford. We're on a quiet street with wonderful neighbors, and we do our part to be equally agreeable. A tall cedar fence encloses our entire backyard. It keeps our dogs safe and also give them plenty of room to run and play where they won't be a bother to anyone else.

"Mom-mee's home!" Kevin came running when I opened the door and walked inside. Faith and Eve were right behind him. For a moment, I was delighted by the warm reception. Usually my comings and goings merit no notice at all. Then Kevin ruined it by adding, "Now we can eat!"

Eat? It was barely past five o'clock. Not only that, but having just arrived, I had yet to make any preparations for dinner.

"Whoa!" I said as Kevin launched himself up into my arms. Then I realized that Bud had appeared and was nipping at my son's heels. "Cut that out," I told the little dog.

"Yeah," Kev echoed, looking down over my shoulder. "Cut it out."

"Cut what out?" Aunt Peg asked, coming into the hallway. She glanced around at the three dogs and knew better than to blame the Poodles. Her gaze fastened on Bud. "You know if you'd take the time to train that dog, he wouldn't always be in trouble."

"I've tried," I told her. *Believe me, I'd tried.* "Bud is training resistant."

"What's that?" Kev asked as he slid down out of my arms.

"It means Bud doesn't listen to what anyone says. He just does whatever he wants."

Kevin's eyes lit up. He'd never previously known that was an option. "I'm training resistant, too," he announced.

"No, you're not," Davey showed up from the direction of the living room. "You're just little."

"Am not!" Kevin stamped his foot.

"Are too." Davey grinned.

Sam appeared in the doorway at the end of the hall that led to the kitchen and looked at me. "I'd say welcome home, but just so you know, I had everything pretty much under control around here until you arrived."

"Big words." I took off my coat and hung it in the

closet, then took my time greeting Faith and Eve properly. "I'd like to see proof." I turned back to Aunt Peg. For some reason, she was cradling Bud in her arms. Maybe she was trying to teach him manners telepathically. "And you," I said. "What are you doing here?"

"I came for dinner," she told me.

"Peg *brought* dinner," Sam added. "Chinese take-out. Including all your favorites."

That was suspicious. "You want something," I said to her.

"Of course I want something," Aunt Peg replied tartly.

Sam nodded toward the boys before she could elaborate.

Oh. I should have realized.

Aunt Peg had heard about Gregory Willet's murder. Given that I'd once again found myself right in the middle of things, she'd come to get the inside scoop. Or given her propensity for ferreting out information—witness her knowledge that I was involved—maybe she'd come to give me a scoop.

With Aunt Peg, you never knew.

I turned to the boys. "Davey, why don't you take Kevin upstairs and the two of you can work on your homework before we eat?"

"I'm in kindergarten," Kevin said. "I don't have any homework."

"Then help Davey with his."

Davey frowned. "That's not help." Nevertheless, he looped his arm around Kevin's shoulders and they headed for the steps. "Come on, squirt. The grown-ups are trying to get rid of us."

"Why?" His frown matched his brother's. "So they can eat all the dumplings while we're gone?"

"Yeah, something like that."

Kevin immediately tried to turn around, but Davey's arm kept him moving forward. Bud, back on the floor again, scampered along behind them.

"We're not eating any dumplings until you get back," I called after them.

"Whatever," Davey said.

Our house has a formal dining room, but we're an informal family, so we usually end up eating our meals at the big, round table in the kitchen. Aunt Peg knew the drill. She went straight to the table, pulled out a chair, and sat down. As Sam unpacked the bags of food and emptied the containers into bowls, I got out drinks, silverware, and napkins.

Faith and Eve followed us into the kitchen. Once they decided no one was working on their food, the two big Poodles lay down in a corner out of the way. The two male Poodles, Tar and Augie, both appeared to be MIA.

"Outside," Sam said, when he saw me looking around. It's convenient to have a man who can read your mind.

I glanced out the nearest window. The outdoor lights were on, so I could see almost the entire backyard. The two dogs were happily wrestling over a length of knotted rope. I figured they'd let us know when they wanted to come in.

"Gregory Willet," Aunt Peg said. Apparently she'd tired of waiting for me to start the conversation.

"He's dead," I told her.

"I know that. I also know you were the one who found his body."

I looked at Sam. He shrugged.

We'd had a discussion about the situation the night before. Generally, Sam is good about keeping things to himself, but he's putty in Aunt Peg's hands. Come to think of it, so is pretty much everyone else.

"A knife in the back, I believe?" she prompted.

"I don't know much more about it than you do," I said.

"It's been more than twenty-four hours. What's keeping you?"

"School. Family. Dogs. You know . . . life."

Aunt Peg wasn't satisfied with that answer. "What about the Chow?" Naturally, she'd be concerned for the dog.

"Mr. Willet's assistant is currently managing the store, and he's also taken custody of Cider. At least until everything gets sorted out. It was a good thing

Trevor stepped in, because it saved the dog from being picked up by Animal Control."

"Cider," Aunt Peg mused. "Not a bad name for a Chow. I hope he wasn't injured in the fracas?"

"No, he was locked away in the storeroom. And as for a fracas, there didn't seem to be much of one. Nothing was broken or appeared to be out of place. Mr. Willet was sitting at the desk in his office when he was stabbed. It looked as though the killer must have taken him by surprise."

"Where was the assistant when that took place?"

"Trevor works afternoons. Mr. Willet was already dead by late morning."

"Pity," Aunt Peg said. "Suspects?"

I shrugged. "Right now, I'm just trying to gather more information about Mr. Willet's life."

"You're no fun," she told me.

Like that was news.

Sam was starting to carry the serving bowls over to the table. Everything smelled wonderful. My stomach rumbled audibly. Before Aunt Peg could pose another question, I left the kitchen and walked to the foot of the stairs.

"Davey, Kevin, dinner's on the table!"

Kevin must have been sitting near the top of the staircase because he was halfway down before I'd even turned away. "It's about time," he said.

Chapter
Nine

On Wednesday, Kevin had a playdate after school. His friend's mother would be picking up both kids at Howard Academy when kindergarten was dismissed, and Sam had offered to retrieve Kev later in the day.

That left me free for the afternoon, which was great because I had things to do. The next time Aunt Peg dropped by with questions, I wanted to have better answers ready.

It had occurred to me that Mr. Willet's neighbor problems might have extended beyond those he'd faced at home. Shoppers at his store dealt with the same issue that plagued most of downtown Greenwich—not enough parking. The tiny lot between Willet's store and the salon next door had just four spaces. On an average day, I suspected salon patrons took over the majority of those spots. Not only that, but they were also likely to hold them for an hour or more—much longer than someone who was just dashing into the pet supply store to buy a box of biscuits.

It was worth looking into whether there'd been any friction between Gregory Willet and the salon owner over the situation. At the same time, I could also find out if anyone at the business next door had seen or heard anything suspicious on the morning of the murder.

When Faith and I pulled up outside the salon at midday, there weren't any open spaces nearby. I drove around the corner to a side street, where I was lucky to find a spot beneath a tree.

"I won't be gone long," I said to Faith as I opened the Volvo's rear windows at the top. The outside temperature was in the fifties, normal for that time of year. "You'll be fine here."

The Poodle's head drooped. She knew what that meant.

I took a rawhide bone out of the glove compartment and held it up. Faith sniffed the air delicately. When I offered her the toy, she deigned to take it from my hand. By the time I'd locked the car, she was already lying down on the seat with her prize.

The salon was named Deluxe Beauty. A small sign out front listed a full range of available services for hair, nails, and skin care, plus massages, waxing, and aromatherapy. Their motto was Look and Feel Your Best Every Day!

If only, I thought. On a range from zero to deluxe, most days I was willing to settle for "pretty good" in both categories. My hair was clean and brushed and my outfit was fine, but I couldn't remember the last time I'd had a manicure or a massage.

The first thing I noticed when I entered the salon was the scent of pumpkin spice in the air. That time of year, it seemed to be everywhere. Beyond that, the place was bustling with activity. Every station in the front was full. Stylists were moving in time to music playing in the background as they worked on clients' hair or nails. There was a constant hum of conversation.

The large room was decorated in shades of cream and gray with black accents. The furniture and fixtures were all outsized and featured sharp angles. The effect was edgy and modern. Gazing around, I felt my assessment of my own appeal plummeting from pretty good to barely adequate.

"May I help you?" A young woman who looked like she'd been airbrushed to perfection was standing behind a front counter.

"Yes. I'd like to speak with the manager, please."

"Of course." Her lips pursed in a small frown. "May I ask what this is in reference to?"

I quickly sorted through several possible replies, then chose the one that seemed most likely to grant me an interview on short notice. "The unexpected death of your neighbor."

"Excuse me?" She blinked. A single purple fingernail began to tap up and down on the countertop. It was long enough to stab someone with. I gulped at the thought.

"Your neighbor," I said. "Gregory Willet?"

She still looked perplexed. But she picked up the receiver on the intercom, pushed a button, then spoke into it. "Stash, there's someone here to see you."

Stash?

"I don't know. She didn't give her name."

Only because I hadn't been asked for it.

Her voice dropped to a whisper. "It's about the pet store guy."

A moment later, she hung up. "He'll be right out," she said brightly, obviously pleased that I was about to become someone else's problem.

Less than a minute passed before a slender man with chiseled features and a full head of black curls came striding toward us from the back of the salon. He was wearing a charcoal gray suit, with a dress shirt that was untucked and had more buttons open than fastened. The heels of his shoes clicked on the floor as he approached.

Before he reached me, the man's hand was already

outstretched. "Hello, I'm Stash Delorean. Deluxe is my salon. How may I help you?"

"I'm Melanie Travis," I said. His skin was soft, but his grip was firm. "I'd like to talk to you about Gregory Willet's murder."

His gaze slid up and down my body. Not in a creepy way. It was more like a *wherever did she get those clothes?* kind of appraisal. Frankly, considering the surroundings, it felt like I deserved that.

"Reporter?"

"No."

Though he quickly hid it, he seemed disappointed by my answer. "Police?"

"No."

Unexpectedly Stash grinned. "Well, now you have me intrigued. Let's go back to my office, shall we?"

People watched us surreptitiously as we walked the length of the salon. I wondered how often visitors got invited back to Stash's office. No doubt it was the mention of an inconvenient murder that had earned me a trip to the private room.

Compared to the luxury out front, Stash's office was plainly furnished, almost spartan. The rug on the floor was threadbare. The desk was made of metal, as was a matching visitor's chair. The leather chair behind the desk looked worn and faded. A window in the rear wall overlooked a dumpster behind the building. The only bright spots in the room were the posters on the walls, each featuring a famous model, a posh locale, and elaborately coiffed hair.

In the salon's outer room, Stash had appeared to be every inch the successful businessman. Here in his office, things were more casual. He doffed his jacket and slung it over the back of the desk chair.

"Have a seat," he said. "May I take your coat?"

"No, I'm fine. Thanks." The office was cooler in temperature than the salon had been. I was just as happy to leave it on.

Stash sat down behind his desk, clasped his hands together on the blotter like an eager student, and gazed at me expectantly. "What can I do for you, Ms. Travis?"

"Hopefully answer a few questions about your neighbor."

He nodded and waited for me to continue.

"How well did you know Mr. Willet, and do you have any thoughts about why someone would have wanted to harm him?"

"I'd consider a knife in the back to be more than just harmful," he said.

"I wasn't aware that the police had released that information."

I'd read every media report I could find. None had specified the exact manner of Willet's death.

Stash shrugged. "People talk. Every business owner along this section of the road has been gossiping about what happened. Naturally, we're all curious. I don't remember who it was that let that information slip."

Or perhaps Stash had known because he was there.

"Your businesses share a common parking lot," I said.

"Yes." He smiled. His teeth were white and even. "So?"

"The space seems quite small to accommodate both your businesses' needs. I wondered if that's ever been a problem for you."

"Of course it's a problem." His smile faded. "Less so for me than for Greg. He and I had several conversations about the inconvenience of sharing an inadequate space."

"Conversations or arguments?"

"Let's say they were discussions that occasionally became heated. Greg wanted to put up signs on two of the spots, indicating that they were only for customers of his store."

"And you disagreed with that idea?"

"Of course I did. It would have been stupid to let the spaces sit empty at times when business at his store was slow. Especially when I have patrons who need to park their vehicles several blocks away." Stash leaned back in his chair and considered me through narrowed eyes. "You never did say. If you're not a reporter and you're not from the police, why are you so interested in what happened to Greg?"

"I was there after he was stabbed," I told him. "I'm the one who found his body."

If I had been hoping for a word of condolence, I would have been disappointed. Stash just nodded. "Bad timing on your part," he said.

"Indeed. Your salon is probably no more than thirty feet from Willet's store. Did you see or hear anything unusual that morning?"

"What time?"

I thought back. "Say, before eleven-thirty?"

He didn't stop to think before replying. "No. The salon opens at ten-thirty, and I don't usually roll in until about an hour later. I probably wasn't even on the premises then."

Probably? We were talking about an event that had taken place just two days earlier. I'd have thought he'd be able to remember exactly when he arrived at work on Monday morning. Especially under these circumstances.

"I'm still not sure why you care about this," Stash said, "but since you do, you should know that you're looking for answers in the wrong place."

"Oh?" I looked at him with interest.

"Greg was having money problems."

"How do you know that?"

He lifted a hand and waved it above his head, then

in the general direction of Willet's store. "These two buildings and the lot between them are a single parcel. They're owned by the same person. Len Crater." He paused for a smirk. "He calls himself Crater Commercial Management, but it's really just one guy."

I looked around Stash's bare-bones office, then glanced back toward the oh-so-chic salon. "It seems he isn't the only one who realizes that putting up a good front matters."

"Touché." Stash grinned, unabashed. "Anyway, Greg hasn't made a rent payment since summer and Len's pretty fed up. He had already served Greg notice of his intent to evict. If Greg didn't hurry up and pay, Len was going to file a complaint with the court next."

"And you think I should talk to Len Crater," I said.

"I would if I were you." Stash pushed back his chair and rose to his feet, signaling my time was up. "He's been hassling Greg for money for months now. Maybe Len got fed up and lost his temper."

"Thanks for the tip," I said.

"Don't mention it." Stash headed for the office door. I stood up and followed. "You ever want to get your nails done, Bibi here is the best in the business. Seeing as you're a friend of the owner, the first manicure is on the house."

"When did we become friends?" I asked as we

walked back through the salon. Once again people stared, some more discreetly than others.

"About the time you called me pretentious," he said over his shoulder.

"I don't remember doing that."

"Sure you do, Melanie Travis. You just couched it in nicer words and hoped I wouldn't notice."

Stash opened the salon's outer door and waited until I'd walked through. "Len Crater," he said. "Don't forget."

The shortest way back to my car took me in front of the pet supply store again. Earlier I'd peered through the windows as I walked by. This time the door opened as I approached, and Trevor Pine came out. He had Cider on a leash beside him.

"Nice to see you again," he said, giving me a little wave.

"You, too. How are things going at the store?"

"Still busy, which is a good thing. I finally got a little break, so I figured I'd bring Cider outside for a walk."

The Chow looked happy to be out of the store. He immediately crossed the sidewalk and began to sniff at a scraggly bush near the curb.

Trevor nodded toward the salon. "I guess you were talking to Stash?"

"Yes." I didn't feel the need to elaborate. Instead I kept walking. Faith would be waiting for me.

"Did he tell you about his feud with Mr. Willet?"

Dammit. I stopped. Then turned. "No, actually, he didn't. Why don't you fill me in?"

"It was over this dumb little lot."

When Cider dragged Trevor away, I had no choice but to follow. "Stash mentioned something about that. He said there was a conversation."

"Hunh," Trevor grunted. "Not likely. The lot is supposed to be split between the two businesses. Two parking spots for them, and two for us. Except that was never how it worked out. Our customers were always complaining about it. Mr. Willet said it cost him business. How would you like to buy a fifty-pound bag of kibble, then have to carry it two blocks to get to your car?"

"I wouldn't," I agreed.

"For years, it wasn't a problem. The building where the salon is now was empty much of the time. Tenants came and went. Nobody seemed to stick, until Stash came along and threw a lot of money at the place. And then suddenly he wanted everything his own way."

Cider was sniffing along the side of the building. Trevor let out the leash and turned back to me. "Mr. Willet wasn't about to give in, especially since he had seniority because his store had been here forever. He put up signs making it clear where the salon patrons were allowed to park and where they weren't."

"Did he?" That was different from the version I'd just heard. Stash had implied that Mr. Willet had conceded to his point of view. Then he'd promptly changed the subject—and I'd been dumb enough to let him get away with it.

"Sure. I helped him make them. We hung them up together." Trevor shook his head. "They didn't even last a whole day. As soon as Stash saw them, he tore them down. Mr. Willet was really angry about that."

"What did he do?" I asked.

"He marched over to the salon and read Stash the riot act. In front of his customers and everything. Neither one of them was about to back down. I heard they nearly came to blows."

"And yet," I said, gesturing at the wall, "Mr. Willet must have given in. Because I don't see any signs."

"I know. That's weird, right?" Trevor frowned. "Mr. W. said he fixed the problem, but I don't know how that can be true." His gaze shifted back to the salon. "Of course, it doesn't matter now, does it? Stash can do whatever he wants. He doesn't have to worry about Mr. Willet anymore."

Chapter
Ten

On our way home, Faith and I stopped at Alice's house. When she and I lived down the street from each other, we'd been in and out of each other's homes all the time. Now it felt as though we didn't get to see each other nearly often enough.

"What? No pumpkin lattes?" Alice said when she came to the door and saw my empty hands. Then she laughed.

"What's so funny?" I waited for Faith to run ahead and greet Berkley, then let myself inside.

"Did you know you can make your own pumpkin spice mix?"

Actually, no. I'd never thought about it.

"This time of year, I put pumpkin spice in just about everything," Alice continued. "And speaking of which, how about a muffin? They just came out of the oven."

"Count me in," I said.

We had at least an hour to ourselves before her teenagers, Joey and Carly, would be home. That felt like a rare luxury. Alice and I headed to the kitchen together. Nobody stood on ceremony in Alice's house. I'd be expected to find a seat and help myself. When she put a basket of muffins in the middle of the table, I could already smell the cinnamon sugar topping. We both sat down and grabbed a muffin.

Faith and Berkley followed us into the kitchen, then lay down on the floor within easy distance of any spillage. Faith put her head between her paws and relaxed. Not Berkley. Judging by the avaricious expression on the Golden Retriever's face, he was thinking about grabbing the muffin out of my hand.

"Don't mind him," Alice said, as she broke off a piece and popped it in her mouth. "Berkley talks a big game, but he usually minds his manners."

"I'm not worried." Thanks to Bud, I was accustomed to dogs who begged at the table with sad faces and hungry eyes. I'd ignore him for now, then probably end up splitting the last piece between him and Faith.

Alice looked at me across the table. "You look better," she commented.

I stopped chewing. "Than what?"

"Two days ago. Then, you were so pale it made me worry. You looked like you'd seen a ghost."

"Then, I nearly had," I pointed out.

"What about since? Has your life returned to normal? Or at least as normal as things ever get around you?"

"That sounds like an insult," I said. "I might resent it if it wasn't true."

"Oh please." Alice wasn't repentant in the slightest. "You know what I mean. You like the rush that chasing down clues and figuring everything out gives you. If you didn't, you wouldn't keep doing it."

I'd never thought of it that way before. "You might be right."

"Of course I'm right." Alice's first muffin had disappeared. She didn't even pause before reaching for another. "I'm a mother."

I was a mother, too. And according to my kids, I was often wrong. Which just went to show how little they knew.

"Hurry up." Mouth full, Alice gestured toward the basket. "You're falling behind."

"Yes, Mom."

She glared. I laughed. After a moment, Alice joined in. That made Faith and Berkley both lift their heads.

"Now look what you've done," I said. "You've disturbed the dogs."

"Shut up and eat," Alice retorted. So I did.

Ten blissful minutes and two muffins later, it was time to get down to business. "I need to ask you something," I said.

"You mean this isn't a social call?" Alice tried to look surprised. Neither of us was fooled.

"Monday when I was here, you reacted when I mentioned Gregory Willet's name." I paused in case Alice wanted to say something. She didn't. "What was that about?"

Her gaze skittered up and down, then sideways. It went pretty much anywhere but in my direction. "This is why you're good at what you do. Because you notice the little things."

I reached for another muffin and split it between our two plates. "And also because I don't let people dodge my questions when I'm trying to get information from them." I trained my eyes on her. "Especially not when they're friends and something makes me wonder if I should be concerned."

"There's nothing for you to worry about." Alice eyed the piece of muffin on her plate, but let it sit for the time being. "Greg Willet is just someone I used to know. So when you brought up his name, I was surprised. And then you said he was dead. Which came as a bit of a shock."

I nodded.

She bit down on her lip. "I didn't want to talk about it then. I guess I needed some time to process what I was feeling."

"I get that," I said. "And I don't mean to pry. So if it's still too soon . . ."

"It's not." Alice shook her head. "But first you have to tell me something. Are you asking as a detective or as a friend?"

"A friend," I said quickly. Then I thought for a moment and held up my hand, thumb and index finger less than an inch apart. "With maybe just a smidge of detective on the side."

Alice eyed my fingers with a frown. "It's that smidge that concerns me."

"Why?" I lowered my hand. "You didn't kill him."

"Of course not," Alice agreed. She stuffed a big piece of muffin into her mouth. "But that doesn't mean I didn't want to. You know. Once upon a time."

I stared at her across the table. Obviously I knew nothing. But I was definitely eager to find out.

"Not that I'd have done the deed myself," she continued. "Especially not with a knife. *Yuck*. No, I would have hired somebody. Maybe a guy with a gun . . . or a woman who was well versed in poisons . . ."

Alice must have noticed the expression on my face because she abruptly stopped talking. "Seriously? You've never wanted to murder someone?"

Okay. She had me there.

"See? It's a perfectly natural impulse. Who was yours?"

"Bob," I admitted.

"Ex-husband Bob?"

I nodded.

"That makes sense," she said. "Considering."

Alice didn't need to fill in the blanks. I knew what she meant.

Considering that Bob had decided he was tired of being married to me when Davey was just ten months old. He'd gotten in his car and driven away without saying good-bye to either of us. Bob had left me with a baby, a mortgage, and a teaching job that was barely adequate to cover even our most pressing expenses.

A lot of time had passed since then, and eventually Bob and I had managed to reconcile our differences. We shared a son, after all, and it was important for Davey's sake that we got along. But those earlier years when I'd felt bereft, abandoned, and overwhelmed by the enormity of how his desertion would impact not just me, but also our son? Absolutely, I'd wanted to kill Bob. I'd have done it in a heartbeat.

Water under the bridge now. *Thank God.*

"Who was Greg Willet to you?" I asked.

Alice pulled in a deep breath, then slowly let it out. "Greg was my fiancé. The man I was madly in love with. He was supposed to be my happily ever after."

My eyes widened as she spoke. Of all the things I'd thought she might say, that wasn't even on the list.

"But Joe—" I blurted out, then stopped.

Alice and her husband, Joe, would celebrate their

twentieth anniversary next year. They were a wonderful couple, totally devoted to each other and their children. Their marriage was one of the best I'd ever seen. It never would have crossed my mind that Joe had been Alice's second choice.

"Joe and I got together later," Alice said. "After Greg broke my heart."

"I'm so sorry." My lower lip wobbled in solidarity. "Whatever went wrong, I know you didn't deserve it."

"*I'm* not sorry," she replied firmly. "In hindsight, Greg dumping me for another woman was the best thing that could have happened."

"Really?" I hoped she meant that.

"Of course. Think about it, Melanie. I have two wonderful kids and a great husband. My life is pretty damn near perfect. Except for when the wonderful kids and the great husband are doing things that drive me crazy. Which is pretty much every day. But still. You know what I mean."

I totally did. We smiled together.

"None of that would have happened for me if I'd married Greg."

"You don't think he'd have made a good husband?"

"With what I know now? No way. But back then, I was naïve. When I was with Greg, I had stars in my eyes. Right up until the day he broke our engagement and asked for his ring back."

I growled under my breath. "I hope you threw it in his face."

"I wish. In the moment, I was so stunned that I just wrestled the ring off my finger and handed it over."

"The woman he dumped you for . . . was it Julia Geist?"

Alice nodded. "Do you know her?"

"We've met. If it's any consolation, her marriage to Willet didn't last long. Nowhere near your twenty years with Joe."

"I know," Alice said, rising from her seat. "After all those muffins, I need something to drink. How about some ice water?"

She and I used to drink soda. Now we were trying to be more health conscious. Half a dozen pumpkin spice muffins notwithstanding.

"Sounds good," I said. "And what do you mean you know?"

"Exactly that." Alice took two glasses out of a cabinet. "Do you think you're the only person around here who's curious about stuff? When Greg left, I wanted to know everything about the woman he'd chosen over me. Through the years, I've engaged in a little social media stalking." She shrugged. "Or maybe more than a little. There's no harm in that, right?"

That sounded like a trick question. Also one I didn't need to answer.

Instead I said cautiously, "Julia seems nice enough."

Alice was standing at the refrigerator, filling two glasses with cold water. She turned and stared at me over her shoulder. "Nice? You're kidding, right?"

No. But obviously I couldn't admit that now.

"Greg didn't leave me for 'nice.' He left me for rich. Greg was the kind of guy who always had his eye on the prize. And apparently I wasn't worth enough for him."

"It sounds as though you're well rid of him . . ." I started to say.

Then it occurred to me that everyone was rid of Greg Willet now. I was starting to think his death hadn't been a huge loss.

"I won't argue with you about that." Alice returned to the table with both glasses. She slid one over to me. "Although, regarding the brevity of their marriage, I don't think Greg was the only one to blame."

"Julia told me that he cheated on her," I said. "Repeatedly."

"Maybe he did. I don't know about that. But Julia seems like a piece of work herself. She's got money and that gives her power. She's not above throwing her weight around to get whatever she wants."

I sipped my water before replying. "Based on the things I've read, Julia's involved in some great causes. She's out there saving whales and working to protect the environment, while half the time I'm so busy I don't even get home in time to make dinner for my family."

"Lucky you." Alice smiled. "You have Sam."

"Not my point," I grumbled, then added. "But point taken."

"Look," she said, "I'm not trying to denigrate Julia Geist. Maybe she's actually a wonderful person. All I'm saying is I've gotten the impression that her public persona and her private one don't line up. Just be careful around her, okay? I think that woman isn't what she seems to be."

That night, after Kevin was in bed and Davey was in his room chatting with his friends on his phone, Sam and I snuggled together on the couch in the living room. Bud was upstairs on Kevin's bed, and the Poodles were asleep around us. It was a rare moment of peace in our house.

"Want to watch some TV?" Sam asked. The remote was on the table in front of us.

"No." I scooted over and leaned my head on his shoulder. "I just want to enjoy the quiet for a few minutes."

"Okay." Sam looped his arm around me and pulled me closer. "How was your day?"

"Busy." I sighed. "But I got to spend some time with Alice. She told me I was lucky to have you."

"Yes," Sam agreed.

I lifted my head and looked at him. "Yes? That's all you have to say?"

"Why would I argue with that?" He grinned. "She's right."

"You're lucky to have me too," I muttered into his chest.

"Yes," he said again.

"You're just waiting for this conversation to end so you can reach for the remote, aren't you?"

"Maybe." At least he had the grace to sound sheepish.

"Is one of your cop shows on?"

"Could be." As if Sam didn't know the schedule of his favorite shows by heart. Still holding on to me, he leaned forward and picked up the device. "I was thinking we might watch together."

I'd only managed to get about one minute of quiet. Even so, this didn't sound like the worst option. I snuggled even closer. Sam's chest was warm and firm. It felt like coming home. I unbuttoned two buttons on his shirt and slipped my hand inside.

"I might fall asleep," I warned him.

"If you do, I'll carry you up to bed."

I could live with that deal.

Chapter
Eleven

The next morning, I dropped Kevin off at his kindergarten classroom, then got Faith settled on her bed in mine. After that, I went in search of Harriet. I found her in the first place I looked, which sounds luckier than it was.

Though classes weren't due to begin for twenty minutes, Mr. Hanover's assistant was already seated behind her desk, prepared for whatever the day might bring. In the event of a zombie apocalypse, Harriet would probably make her last stand outside the headmaster's office. She guarded Mr. Hanover, and his inner sanctum, with relentless dedication.

"Good, you're here," she said. Today her cashmere sweater set was sky blue and she wore matching blue topaz studs in her ears. She gestured toward a straight-backed chair nearby. "Sit."

The chair was where I usually perched nervously when I was called to the headmaster's office to account for some transgression I'd committed. I lowered myself into the seat and wondered why Harriet sounded as though she'd been expecting me.

"Cookie?" She extended a plate in my direction. Harriet's marshmallow puffs were legendary, but those were a Halloween treat. Now that it was November, it appeared that we'd moved on.

"Pumpkin spice?" I guessed, as I helped myself.

"Of course. In keeping with the theme of our fundraiser, what else would I serve visitors? And speaking of which, I assume you came to hear the latest figures?"

"Sure." I sat back and nibbled on my cookie, feeling marginally better. When I was in trouble, Harriet never offered me sweets.

She and I had planned the fundraiser together, but due to my other responsibilities, she was the person in charge of its execution. Ten days in, Harriet had a running tally of how many tokens our students had collected, both individually and by grade. Another file tracked donations from parents and local businesses. A third listed the prizes we'd be awarding at the end. Even though the treasure hunt was in progress, new contributions continued to trickle in.

"Fourth grade is currently in the lead," she said. "With sixth not far behind. Melissa Peabody is our individual leader." Harriet peered closely at her computer screen. "That child is ahead by a mile."

"It's not surprising. Melissa's one of the most competitive students I've ever met." I lowered my voice before continuing. "And the parents don't help. Melissa is nine and already talking about Harvard. Like it's a given that's where she'll go. Her teacher and I are trying to dial back the pressure, but that only works when she's in school."

Harriet nodded. "Maybe this contest will help. Give her something to take her mind off her studies."

"Or something else to stress about."

"Those are my updates," Harriet said. She was ready to move on. "Now let's hear yours. I'm assuming you have something to tell me."

"Yes and no."

"Yes and yes would be a better answer." She offered the plate of cookies again, and I took another. "It's been almost three days. I hope you've been busy."

I was tempted to stuff the whole cookie in my mouth so I'd have an excuse not to answer. I wished I had more news for her. Or maybe just better news.

"I've spoken with a couple of Greg Willet's neighbors," I said. "Apparently he'd been embroiled in disputes over dogs and parking spaces."

Harriet didn't bother to question that odd pairing. She and I had known each other for a long time. Virtually everything I did ended up involving dogs in one way or another. And parking? It was Greenwich. Parking was always a problem.

"I also spoke with Willet's ex-wife. Her name is Julia Geist. Maybe you've heard of her?"

Harriet nodded, which wasn't surprising. Considering the number of local events and charities Julia was involved in, it would have been more surprising if she hadn't. Harriet began to shuffle through some papers on her desk. After a moment, she found what she was searching for.

"Did you say something to Julia Geist about our fundraiser?" she asked.

"Just very briefly." I thought back. "And only in the context that Willet's store was involved. I did mention that I work at Howard Academy, though. Is there a problem?"

"No." Harriet looked bemused. She was staring at a list of numbers in her hand. "Not unless you think a five-figure donation is a problem."

"Five figures?" It took me a second to compute that. That was at least ten thousand dollars. "From Julia Geist?"

"Indeed. It came in yesterday."

"The day after she and I spoke. How very strange."

I sat back in the chair, trying to figure out what that meant.

Harriet put two and two together faster than I did. "How amiable was her relationship with her ex?"

"Not at all. Willet was a bad husband and a bad father. Plus, they had money issues that continued to be a problem even after their divorce."

"Hush money," Harriet said.

"Excuse me?"

I'd heard what she said. But the idea seemed so far-fetched, I wanted her to repeat it anyway.

"Hush money." She smacked her lips in satisfaction. "You know, a bribe, a kickback, a little payola on the side."

Even though this was serious business, I found myself laughing. "Payola" was not the kind of word I'd ever expected to hear coming out of the very proper administrative assistant's mouth. Plus, Harriet had to be overstating the situation. *Didn't she?*

"Surely you don't think Julia Geist's donation to Howard Academy is meant to buy my silence?" I said.

"Of course I do." Harriet slid a knowing look in my direction. "Don't you?"

At one o'clock, Sam came by the school to pick up Kevin and Faith. The three of them were on their way to get ice cream, my son informed me gleefully. Faith looked equally pleased by the prospect.

The idea sounded so good that I was almost tempted to join them. Except that now, in addition to everything else, Harriet was ramping up her demand for answers. That meant I'd be heading in the opposite direction, unfortunately.

Crater Commercial Management listed an address on the Post Road in Byram, a section of Greenwich that bordered New York State. I arrived there to find myself at a tiny strip mall offering just three stores: a barbershop, a shoe repair shop, and the Crater Management office.

When I parked my car out front, I could see the entirety of Len Crater's place of business through the grimy window that took up three-quarters of the front wall. The office was just one room, and it wasn't much to look at. Stark fluorescent lighting threw the single desk, bare walls, and linoleum floor into sharp relief. A couch that looked like it might have been found by the side of the road was shoved along one wall.

The good news, however, was that there was a man sitting at the desk, talking on his phone. Len Crater, I presumed. When I pushed the door open and walked inside, he swiveled in his chair and looked at me in surprise. Like maybe he'd never had a visitor drop by before.

"Hey, gotta go," he said into the phone. "Call you later."

He put the device down on the desk and rose to his feet. Len was five foot eight and stocky. He was maybe fifty in age, and already mostly bald. Dressed in a pair of rumpled khakis topped by an equally wrinkled button-down shirt, he looked about three days since his last shave. He had a pair of scuffed Topsiders on his feet.

"Len Crater," he said, swaggering toward me with a misplaced sense of his own importance. "What can I do you for?"

There's a certain kind of man who finds that opening funny. Indeed, Len was already smiling at his own wit. When I was six, I might have found it amusing too. Now I ignored it and mustered a pleasant expression. I was, after all, hoping he'd help me out by answering my questions.

"I'm Melanie Travis," I said. "I'd like to talk to you about one of your tenants."

"Must be Greg Willet." Crater shook his head. "That guy's the man of the hour. Everybody wants to talk about him."

It didn't take a genius to figure out why. Though, judging by what I'd seen so far, that still might have been beyond Crater's capabilities.

I expected him to inquire about the source of my interest in Willet's death, but he didn't bother. Maybe because he appeared to be having a slow day. Could be Crater was hoping I'd liven up his afternoon. I was definitely hoping he'd have information that would enhance mine.

He waved expansively in the direction of the couch. "Have a seat. Make yourself at home."

I inched in that direction, taking a closer look before perching gingerly on the edge of the cushion. I hoped I didn't pick up fleas. Faith would never forgive me.

Crater went around behind his desk and sat down again. "So," he said, "what do you want to know?"

I led with the question that was uppermost in my mind. "Why would someone want to kill Mr. Willet?"

"Beats me." Crater's shoulders rose and fell in an elaborate shrug. Then he snickered. "Pet supplies. Who woulda thought that was a dangerous game?"

"So you think Willet's death was related to his business?"

"Like you want me to guess?" Crater seemed intrigued by the idea.

"Sure," I said. *Why not?*

"Nah, it probably wasn't the business," he decided. "Willet must've gotten himself in some other kind of trouble. Guy was an idiot."

"What makes you say that?"

"'Cause it's true." His head bobbed up and down as he snickered again. It wasn't a good look for a man his age. Not the first time and certainly not the second. "Ask anybody."

I was doing my best. "Is it true he owed you money?"

"Where'd you hear that?"

"Around." I wasn't about to give up my source. Not to this guy, who was also Stash's landlord. "Apparently it's no secret."

"It was that damn Delorean, wasn't it? That hairdresser has a big mouth." Crater smirked. "Guys like him, that's what they do all day. Put their hands in ladies' hair and gab, gab, gab." He mimed scissoring with his fingers. "He ought to try working at a real job."

"He has a real job," I said mildly. "He owns a successful salon."

Crater stared at me. "Did he tell you that?"

"He didn't have to tell me. I saw it for myself."

"Yeah, right." He didn't look impressed. "Delorean's in hock up to his eyeballs. The luxury business is expensive, he tells me. You have to look the part, impress the ladies up front, in order to make money. Just give me a month's grace, and I'll pay you back with interest." Crater growled under his breath. "Damn right you will."

"Are you telling me that both of your tenants are behind on their rent?" I asked, surprised.

"What do you think?" He lifted a hand and waved it around the small room. "Do I look like I'm living the high life here?"

"No." Frankly, considering that Crater was just one man with a desk and a phone, I wondered why he needed an office at all. "I hope your other properties are doing better."

"What other properties?" he snapped, then quickly frowned and shut his mouth. He looked like he was hoping I would change the subject. I decided to oblige him.

"You were taking steps to evict Greg Willet," I said.

"So? What of it? That's what happens when you don't pay your rent."

"Yes, but . . ." Something else he'd just said didn't make sense to me. "It sounds as though you'd extended credit to Stash. Why him and not Willet?"

"Coupla things." Crater crossed his arms over his chest and leaned forward to brace his elbows on the desk. "Willet's Pet Supplies has been in that building for nearly twenty years. He did a five-year renewal on his lease just last year."

I still didn't get it. "So he's a long-term tenant of yours. And presumably someone who's kept up with his rent payments all those years. Both those things should stand him in good stead."

"Sure," Crater allowed. "*If* he was still paying on time. Which he's not. Delorean is a different case entirely. He signed a two-year lease eighteen months ago. It took him half that time to get that business up and running. Guy's put plenty of improvements into that building, and now his lease is nearing its end.

That means he's more nervous about that missing payment than I am. Because you better believe he and I will be square before we sit down to discuss a new lease."

"A *new* lease?" I said. "Shouldn't it be a renewal?"

"Right." Crater grinned wolfishly. "And it would have been if I was dealing with someone who knew what he was doing when it comes to real estate. Then the contract would have had an automatic renewal clause with a specified rate already built in."

Crater looked so pleased with himself, it wasn't hard to figure out what he was getting at. "Stash's lease doesn't have such a clause?"

He shook his head.

"And Willet's did?"

"Sure it did. Not that it matters now."

The backs of my legs were beginning to itch. The sensation had to be psychosomatic. Surely the couch didn't really have fleas. I stood up anyway. Once on my feet, I was tempted to shake like a dog emerging from water. That would probably make me look crazy.

"What if you wanted to sell that property?" I asked.

"Depends," Crater told me. "On whether the buyer wanted the buildings filled with paying tenants, or empty so he could do something else with them. It could go either way."

Except the way it currently was going, I thought. Two buildings with nonpaying tenants had to be the worst possible option. It was also likely to mean that—at least for now—Crater was stuck with his unprofitable investment.

"Have you ever thought about selling?" I asked as I started for the door.

"Sure. I'm in real estate. That's what guys like me do. Wheel and deal all the time. And that's first-rate Greenwich property. Every time you blink, it rises in value. I'd have to be a fool not to think about it."

I bit back the first reply that came to mind. *Wheel and deal, indeed.*

"What will happen to Willet's store now?" I asked instead.

"What are you asking me for? Talk to Willet's heirs."

I wondered if that meant Crater wasn't aware that Greg Willet hadn't been the sole owner of his store. "Who are his heirs?"

"How should I know?" Crater replied. "I guess we'll find out soon enough. Then they'll find out they owe me back rent—and that I intend to collect."

Chapter
Twelve

When I made a second attempt to see him, Greg Willet's neighbor, Erik Poole, was home. There was a car parked in the driveway, and this time when I rang the doorbell, it was answered almost immediately.

"Erik Poole—?" I began.

"Now what?"

The man who'd opened the door was tall and skinny. His shoulders were as narrow as his hips. He had shaggy brown hair and a scruffy beard to match. He jammed his hands into the pockets of his jeans and waited for me to reply.

"I don't know," I said, flustered by the unexpected question. "What does that mean?"

"I've already spoken to the police, regional media, and two national correspondents. Surely all the bases must be covered by now."

"National news?" His answer hadn't helped. I was still confused. "Gregory Willet's death is a national story?"

Erik shrugged. "You can blame the internet for that. The twenty-four hour news cycle is always hungry for new information. So, what's your angle?"

"I don't have an angle."

He leaned against the doorjamb, the nonchalant stance only adding to the impression that he was toying with me. "You must, or you wouldn't be here. Local?"

"Stamford," I replied, then belatedly realized he wasn't asking where I lived, but which news outlet I worked for.

"Good enough," he said, stepping back out of the doorway. "You might as well come in."

The door opened directly into a living room that had been decorated by someone who liked bright colors. Floral prints covered almost everything. The walls were painted apple green, and the carpet beneath our feet was a sunny shade of yellow. It was a bit much to take in all at once.

"My wife designed the room," Erik said. He must have noticed me looking around. "She's at work now."

"Oh?" I sat down on a Scandinavian-style sofa that was more comfortable than it looked. "What does she do?"

"Admin work at a dentist's office." The remark was offhand. "But that's only temporary. Until my book sells."

"Your book?"

"It's a true crime thriller." A smile lit up Erik's face. "Based on events that took place more than a hundred years ago. A real-life historical crime spree. Readers are going to lap it up. There may even be a movie."

"Good for you." I hadn't expected that. "When does your book come out?"

"That remains to be seen." Erik dropped into a chair on the other side of the room. "At the moment, I'm still looking for an agent."

No wonder Erik had been so busy giving interviews. He had a manuscript to sell. This opportunity to build name recognition must have seemed like a real stroke of serendipity.

"True crime," I said. "What are the chances?"

"I know. Right?" He was almost bouncing in his seat. "Maybe this will be my lucky break."

Not so lucky for Greg Willet, I thought.

"Erik Poole." He reminded me of his name. Another minute, and he'd be spelling it for me. "It's a writer's name, don't you think? Short and punchy. It'll look great on a book cover."

"Or a best-seller list," I said.

That earned me an even bigger smile. He was sure we were on the same page now.

"So, what do you need to know?" he asked.

"I want to talk to you about your neighbor."

"Sure, Greg. Great guy."

"Really? That's not what I heard." I took out my phone and set it to record. I figured that was a nice touch.

"Well . . . you know . . . he's dead." Erik adopted a sad face. "So obviously not everyone thought so."

"I understand there was a problem with his dogs?"

"Chow Chows," he said. "You ever seen one of those?"

Chows were in the Non-Sporting Group along with Miniature and Standard Poodles, so I'd seen many of those. But Erik didn't wait for me to reply.

"It's some kind of Chinese breed with hair all over it. They look like lions. One of those things racing at you at full speed is enough to scare a person half to death."

"I can imagine," I said. "Did that happen often?"

"Too often," Erik muttered. "Greg thought of himself as some kind of Chow rescuer. He took in all these dogs that other people had dumped, then tried to find homes for them."

"That sounds like a noble idea."

His eyes narrowed.

"But probably hard to live next to," I added.

"Damn straight. And they bark all the time too. *Woof! Woof! Woof!*" Erik demonstrated, apparently in case I'd never heard a dog bark before.

"That must have been annoying for you."

"Annoying isn't the half of it. I work at home, so I'm here all day. Imagine trying to write a best-seller with all that noise going on next door. Some days, the aggravation was enough to make me want to—"

Abruptly he stopped speaking, then snapped his mouth shut. Too bad. I'd have been interested to hear how that sentence ended.

"I can understand why you were angry," I said.

"In my shoes, anyone would have felt the same way. I even filed a complaint with the police."

That was interesting. "What did they do?"

"Nothing."

"At all?"

"Some cop stopped by and had a talk with Greg, who crossed his heart and promised to do better. Lying scum. He didn't change a thing. The same damn problem continued right up until the day he died."

I remembered what Greg's other neighbor had told me about someone coming to pick up the remaining Chows. "You must have been happy when Greg and his Chows were gone."

"You better believe it," Erik agreed grimly.

* * *

I had one more stop to make before I headed home.

The timing of Julia Geist's donation to the Howard Academy fundraiser felt worrisome to me. Harriet's reference to the gift as "hush money" seemed overly dramatic, but perhaps not entirely unwarranted. If Julia had another motivation for making the significant gift, I wanted to know what it was.

"I'm home now," she said when I called and asked if we could get together. "I'll be here all afternoon. I'll text you the address."

Julia lived in Old Greenwich. Nearing her house, I turned onto the road that led to the beach at Tod's Point. Properties on the water in Greenwich were generally fabulous to look at and had price tags to match. As I'd suspected, Julia Geist's house didn't disappoint.

It was a three-story colonial with a widow's walk in the middle of its peaked roof. Ivy wound around the Doric columns that supported an oversized portico covering the front entrance. Numerous windows sparkled in the autumn sunlight. It was a house with character—imposing without being showy, grand but not ostentatious.

When I parked on the far side of the turnaround, I could see the lawn behind the house. It went back at least a hundred feet before ending at Long Island Sound. From there, a small jetty extended out over the water. The view was stunning.

When I presented myself at the front door, I was quickly admitted to the house by a young woman with long blond hair, delicate features, and a ready smile. "Hi, I'm Lucia," she said. "You must be Ms. Travis. Come on in. My mom's expecting you."

I tried not to gawk as we made our way to an enclosed porch that ran almost the length of the back of the house. It was filled with groupings of wicker and chintz-covered furniture, and decorated with large ferns and a dozen different hanging plants. Despite the cold November breeze blowing off the Sound, the porch was warm and cozy. When I slipped off my coat, Lucia took it from me and hung it on a hook.

"How nice of you to drop by," Julia said, rising gracefully from a settee. A tea tray and a plate of cookies were set out on a table in front of her. "I see you've met my daughter."

"Yes. Although we haven't yet had a chance to talk." I turned and addressed Lucia, who was nabbing a cookie from the plate. "I heard you're job hunting. What kinds of things are you interested in?"

"My bachelor's degree is in early child development, so naturally I'm hoping to find something that allows me to use what I've learned," she told me. "I understand that you work in education too."

"I do. I'm a special needs tutor at Howard Academy. Like your mother, I'm a strong proponent of educational programs that offer young students lots of support and early guidance."

Lucia glanced at Julia, then back to me. "Please tell me if this is an imposition, but I'd love to have the opportunity to come to Howard Academy and shadow you for a day or two. It would be wonderful to be able to watch some of your sessions. I know it would help me decide if that's a career path I should consider following."

"I'd be delighted to have you visit my classroom," I said with a smile. "But before I say yes, I'll need to check with Mr. Hanover, the school's headmaster. I doubt if he'll have any objections, but I'll talk to him and get back to you. Is that okay?"

Lucia squealed happily. "Yes, that's perfect. Thank you so much!"

Seeing how excited her daughter was, Julia was smiling too. "You can run along now, Lulu. Ms. Travis and I have some things to discuss."

"She's lovely," I said when Lucia had left the porch and closed the door behind her. Julia and I took seats across from each other.

"Yes, she is," Julia said fondly. "Smart, too, and eager to do well. I like to think Lucia takes after me, although I suppose I should give Gregory a modicum of credit. Tea?"

"I'll just have a cookie, if that's all right." She nodded and I helped myself. The cookies were oatmeal and liberally studded with fat, juicy raisins. They made a pleasant change from all the pumpkin spice I'd consumed recently.

Julia poured herself a cup of tea, then settled back in her seat. "I assume that whatever you wanted to talk to me about has something to do with my ex. Am I correct?"

"You are. I'd like to thank you for recommending that I speak with his neighbors. It was very helpful. Among other things, Mr. Hamm mentioned that someone came and removed the dogs from Mr. Willet's house. Did you arrange that?"

"No, that was Trevor Pine's doing. He's the young man who's in charge of the store now. It was fortunate he realized that we needed to take responsibility for Gregory's other Chows. Have you met Trevor?"

I nodded and took another bite of my cookie. "Yes, when I was at the store earlier in the week. He told me he's also taking care of Cider. It's great that he was willing to step in."

"Trevor is an industrious young man," Julia said. "I like people who volunteer to be helpful, rather than waiting to be conscripted. Trevor has been a real asset to the business. He's done wonderful things for us on social media. He even shoots the occasional Tik-Tok video in the store."

"It sounds as though you'll be keeping him on as manager."

"I certainly don't foresee making any changes soon." She paused to sip her tea. "Do you have children, Melanie?"

The abrupt change in subject came as a surprise. But I was learning that Julia didn't do anything without a good reason. So I was happy to follow along.

"I have two sons," I told her. "One's fifteen, and the other is five."

"Then you'll understand, as only a mother can, how much your children's happiness means to you. Trevor and Lucia have been seeing each other for nearly a year. They make a truly lovely couple. Privately, I'll admit that I have hopes it could turn into a long term situation. Not that I have any intention of meddling, mind you . . ."

I huffed under my breath. Julia looked over at me and winked.

"But if it happens that their relationship *is* that serious, it wouldn't hurt for Trevor to have a stable job, now would it?"

"Not at all," I agreed.

It occurred to me that Julia was like Machiavelli, pulling strings and manipulating events behind the scenes until people fell into place and did what she wanted them to. The thought might have been alarming. Instead, it suddenly made me feel better as another realization clicked into place. Now I just needed to confirm my guess.

"I wanted to ask you about a donation you made yesterday to the Howard Academy fundraiser," I said.

"What about it?" Julia regarded me over the rim of her teacup.

"First of all, thank you. That was very generous."

"You're welcome. I was happy to do it. I'm sure HA will put the funds to good use."

"They will," I assured her. "Initially, however, the timing of your donation seemed slightly . . . suspicious."

"Did it?" I'd hoped Julia wouldn't be offended. To my relief, she sounded amused. "In what way?"

"Arriving as it did, just one day after you and I had been discussing Mr. Willet's untimely death—"

"You mean his murder."

That was the second time she'd corrected my terminology with regard to the incident. Julia was remarkably blasé about her ex-husband's demise.

"Yes—his murder—which I was looking into. I imagine you can understand how a significant donation coming on the heels of that conversation might be interpreted as an incentive for me to look elsewhere."

"A bribe, then," Julia said.

I winced at the inference, but she still didn't look

perturbed. At least she hadn't called it payola. "Precisely."

"Melanie, the need for better and more accessible education is my most personal cause. I applaud Howard Academy's goals and their accomplishments. Though my timing could have been better, I assure you that the donation arrived with no special conditions attached."

That wasn't entirely true, I thought. Only its condition wasn't the one I'd originally suspected.

"However," I said, "if the donation were to make Mr. Hanover more amenable to the idea of Lucia exploring a career in education by spending time in my classroom at Howard Academy, I assume that would just be a happy coincidence?"

"Indeed it would."

This time when Julia winked at me, I found myself laughing with her.

Chapter
Thirteen

It turned out that Julia's house wouldn't be my last stop for the day. As soon as I got back in my car, my phone began to ring. It was Harriet. I pulled out onto the road and connected the call.

"Hi, Melanie," she said. "Can you do me a favor?"

"Sure. What do you need?"

"Since we spoke this morning, I've received requests for more muffin tokens from four different stores. It's great that supplies are running low, it means our treasure hunt is a big success. But now I'd like to get those tokens replenished as quickly as possible. So I was wondering . . ."

Harriet was always thinking ahead. As usual, it stood her in good stead. "You're wondering if I took your advice and stashed a box of spare tokens in my car. Right?"

"Yes. And fortunately it sounds as though you had the good sense to listen to me." Like Aunt Peg, Harriet couldn't resist taking advantage of a teachable moment. "I know you're currently off the clock."

"Don't worry about it," I said. "I'm still around town. Text me the names of the stores, and I'll get right on it."

While she did that, I drove back out to the Post Road and turned west to head to downtown Greenwich. "One more thing, before you go. I spoke with Julia Geist about her donation," I said.

Harriet made an unhappy noise under her breath. I knew she'd been just as curious about the gift as I was. But considering that Julia was a force in the education community, I was sure she hadn't want me to do anything that might rock the boat. Or possibly sink it entirely.

"I hope you at least tried to be subtle about it," she said. Sadly, she didn't sound hopeful.

"You would hardly have recognized me. I was a paragon of delicacy and nuance."

Harriet groaned. "Now I know we're in trouble."

"No, it's okay." I grinned even though she couldn't see it. "Julia did want something in return, but it's not what we suspected."

"Oh?" That piqued her interest.

As I drove back into Greenwich, I explained about Lucia, her degree in early child development, and her desire for a job that would put the degree to good use. When I got to the part about Lucia shadowing me for a few days, Harriet was immediately enthusiastic about the idea.

"We can make that happen," she said.

"Mr. Hanover won't object?"

"Are you kidding? For a donation that size, he'd probably be willing to send a car and driver to pick her up in the morning and take her home again in the afternoon."

"I don't think we need to go that far."

I turned onto Greenwich Avenue. The town's main shopping district ran all the way from the top of the hill to the railroad tracks at the bottom, several long blocks away. Despite the distance I might have to walk, I immediately began to keep my eye out for an empty space.

"You just leave everything to me," Harriet said. "I'll get the okay from Mr. Hanover and put a plan in motion."

"Harriet, you're a treasure. Howard Academy is lucky to have you."

"I know," she said, and hung up.

The box in the back of the Volvo held one hundred pumpkin spice muffin tokens. When I'd placed it there, I thought the amount was overkill. Now I realized that meant just twenty-five tokens for each of the stores that had asked for additional supplies. I hoped it would be enough to hold them for another week.

As luck would have it, the bakery, the men's clothing store, and the pizza parlor were all within easy walking distance of where I'd parked. The last store on Harriet's list was Willet's Pet Supplies. I felt a guilty pang. I'd been so busy, I'd forgotten Trevor mentioning how quickly he was running through tokens earlier in the week. I probably should have remedied that sooner.

Trevor was behind the counter, checking out a customer, when I entered the store. The woman had a small, fluffy dog in her arms and an imperious expression on her face. After paying for her purchase with a gold credit card, she directed Trevor to bag her items and carry them outside to her car.

He cast me an apologetic look as they walked past. *Be right back,* he mouthed silently.

"No hurry," I replied aloud.

"I should hope not," the woman snapped. Trevor smothered a grin and followed her outside.

Once they were gone, the store was quiet. I didn't see Cider anywhere. When Mr. Willet was in the store, the Chow had usually been on a bed behind the counter. I walked over to take a look and saw that the bed was gone too. Trevor must have had to make another arrangement.

"Sorry about that." Hurrying back inside, Trevor raked a hand through his short hair, making it stand on end. "Mrs. Plimpton assumes the world exists solely for her care and comfort. She's one of the store's best customers, so she's used to Mr. Willet spoiling her with extra attention. I'm lucky she didn't snap her fingers to make me move faster."

"Or make you carry the dog."

"No way that's happening," he said. "Fifi bites."

"Now that you're in charge of the store, maybe Mrs. Plimpton can adapt to a new kind of behavior."

"Old dogs and new tricks?" Trevor laughed. "I don't think so." He eyed the bag of tokens in my hand. "I hope those are for me. I'm almost out."

"They are." When I handed him the bag, he took it and tucked it behind the counter.

"I think I'm having almost as much fun with your treasure hunt as the kids are," he said. "How's the fundraising coming along?"

"It's going great. The idea's been so successful, I think Mr. Hanover might decide to use it again in future years." Mention of the headmaster reminded me of the conversation I'd just had with Julia. "By the way, I met Lucia earlier. I heard you and she are a couple."

"Did she tell you that?" Trevor sounded pleased.

"Actually, her mother did. Lucia seems like a nice girl."

"She is." The tips of his ears went pink. "She's really wonderful. I never thought I'd be lucky enough to meet someone like her."

"It sounded as though Julia is firmly in your corner too," I said.

Trevor nodded. "She told me she likes my work ethic, which is one of the reasons I've tried so hard to make this store a success. I want to be worthy of that regard. When you look at what Julia has accomplished in her life, it's easy to see where Lucia gets her initiative, her intelligence . . . pretty much all her admirable qualities."

"That doesn't give Mr. Willet much credit," I teased.

He just shrugged. "I imagine he contributed something."

I was sure I'd heard a note of discontent. "But?"

"Mr. Willet was the kind of father who thought no one would ever be good enough for his little girl. Lucia and I were working on bringing him around, but truthfully, I'm not sure why his opinion even mattered. If Lucia was so important to him, why did he desert his family all those years ago? Julia's the one who raised Lucia and made her the terrific woman she is."

"That's a lovely sentiment," I told him. "I'm sure Julia would be delighted to hear it."

"She already has," Trevor said with a smile. "More than once. Then Lucia says that while she's happy to agree Julia gave her a wonderful start, I should still acknowledge she's an adult who's responsible for herself and her own achievements."

"Lucia has a point, too," I said.

Trevor shook his head. "This is why men should never argue with women. Because women argue both sides, so they can never lose."

"Or," I countered, "we win because we're better at it."

The door to the store opened behind him. A delivery man came inside, holding out a bill of lading. Visible through the window, a panel truck was idling on the road out front.

"It looks like you have to go," I said.

Trevor turned to look. "Right. Thanks for stopping by. And for the extra tokens. I'll put them to good use."

As he hurried away, I remembered I'd meant to ask him about Cider. Unfortunately, I'd missed my chance.

As I left the store, I paused and glanced at the salon next door. Stash was probably there. I wondered if he wanted to offer an explanation for allegedly tearing down Willet's signs. Or if he wanted to hear about my conversation with his landlord, who'd implied that Stash would be in trouble when it came time to renew his lease.

Either idea alone was interesting. Together, they were enough to send me striding across the small lot in the direction of the salon.

The receptionist with the dagger-like nails didn't look up as I entered. "Name?" she inquired.

"Melanie Travis," I said. Not that I could see how that would help.

Her gaze shifted from the screen on her phone to the screen on an iPad. "You don't have an appointment," she told me with a notable lack of interest. "Sorry, we don't take walk-ins."

"I'm here to talk to Stash. Is he available?"

The woman's head finally lifted. "Stash?"

"The owner," I clarified. As if she didn't know.

I was saved from having to explain further when the man himself came strolling toward us from his office at the back of the salon. "Melanie, how nice to see you." Stash took my hand in his, then glanced down at my unvarnished nails. "Are you here for your manicure?"

"No, I was actually hoping we could talk."

"Again?" His eyes twinkled. Stash was a handsome man and he knew it. "I'm flattered."

Scores of women had probably fallen for that line. I wasn't going to add myself to the list. "I'm not sure you should be."

"And once again, I find myself intrigued," Stash murmured. "Let's go back to my office, shall we?"

"How did you know I was here?" I asked when we'd assumed the same seats we had the day before.

Stash was behind his desk, and I was in the only other chair in the room. Its metal seat was cold and hard. I kept my coat on and resisted the urge to shiver.

"Cameras." He flicked a finger toward his monitor. "When I'm back here, I can see everything that goes on out front. It's a surprisingly useful application. I learn all sorts of unexpected things."

"Do you have cameras outside too?" I asked hopefully.

"Why would—" he began, then stopped. "Oh, I see what you're asking. Sorry, no. I'm afraid I can't help."

"That's too bad. I stopped by to ask you about something else though."

Stash nodded. As if he was an open book. Which I very much doubted.

"The signs that Greg Willet made to indicate where his customers, and yours, were permitted to park their cars."

He steepled his hands on his desk, looking only mildly curious and not like a man who was about to be caught out. "What about them?"

"I heard you were angry when Willet hung them up. And that shortly thereafter, you went out and ripped them down."

"Wait . . . what?" Stash frowned. "Who told you that?"

I ignored the question. I wasn't about to get Trevor in trouble. "Is it true?"

"It's true that I removed the signs. But by the time I took them down, they weren't needed anymore."

I sat back in my chair. The metal slats were cold too. "Meaning what?"

"Greg and I came to an agreement."

"So you're saying that he didn't come over here and yell at you?"

"Oh, yeah." Stash chuckled. "He did do that. Greg had a temper all right."

"Do you have a temper too?" I wondered if he would admit to getting into a fight with a dead man.

"Only when I'm being treated unfairly."

"And Willet's signs were unfair?"

"That's not what I said," Stash corrected me. "The signs were just a stupid idea. So I called Greg and told him I was going to take them down. That's when he came over and yelled at me. And since he'd had the nerve to disrupt my place of business, I yelled back at him. Then we came here to my office and settled things."

"How did you do that?"

"We negotiated an agreement that was fair to both of us." Stash's tone was dry to the point of sarcasm. "Going forward, my customers were allowed to take whatever spaces were available. In exchange, I agreed to pay Greg a sum of money every month for the privilege of using my own parking lot."

"Oh," I said, feeling deflated.

The arrangement didn't sound equitable to me either. I wondered why someone who placed a high value on fairness would agree to it. I didn't have a chance to ask, however, because Stash was already rising from his seat.

"Let me walk you out," he said. It was a toss-up whether he was trying to be gentlemanly, or ensure that I left.

I stood up, then reached out a hand to stop him from leaving the office. "There's something else. I took your advice and spoke with Len Crater. You need to have a real estate lawyer look over the lease agreement you signed with Crater Commercial Management."

Abruptly Stash stopped walking. "How do you know anything about that?"

"Len's a talker. He bragged about the deal he'd made when you took over this property. Its terms are not favorable to you."

Stash's eyes narrowed briefly. Then he quickly resumed his usual confident air. "Thanks for the tip." His hand, pressed gently against the small of my back, guided me out of the salon.

It wasn't until I was out on the sidewalk, heading back to my car, that I was struck by a sudden thought. If Gregory Willet wasn't paying his rent *and* was collecting extra cash on the side, where was all that money going?

Chapter
Fourteen

Friday morning, when Faith and I arrived at our classroom, Lucia was there waiting for us. I'd expected it to take a couple of days for Harriet to set everything up. Obviously I'd underestimated her abilities.

Lucia started to wave a greeting to me, then her gaze dropped to Faith. Immediately, she began to smile. She stooped down and held out her hands. "Who's this?"

"Her name is Faith." As I hung up my coat and put my purse in a desk drawer, the Poodle trotted across the room into Lucia's arms. The two of them wriggled around together, delighted to have made each other's acquaintance. "She's my assistant. Some people might say she's my better half."

"Faith is gorgeous." With her hands still wrapped around the Poodle, Lucia looked up at me. "I always wanted to have a dog of my own."

Considering the way Julia had spoken about her ex-husband's Chows, it wasn't hard to figure out why that had never happened at her primary home.

"What about when you were with your father?" I asked. "He must have liked dogs."

Lucia rose to her feet. "I wasn't at his place very often. So I'd have ended up spending more time away from a dog than with it. Plus, Dad was really into the whole rescue thing, you know?"

I nodded.

"Nothing felt stable at his house. Sometimes it was just chaos. Dogs would leave, then new ones would show up. There were dog bowls on the kitchen table, and dog crates in my bedroom. I never knew what to expect next."

"Divorce is hard on children," I said. "And it's hard on parents when you have children."

Lucia and I pulled out chairs and sat down at one of the round tables in the room. We still had fifteen minutes until my first tutoring session was due to begin. Faith was an empathetic dog. She followed us and sat down next to Lucia's chair, placing herself within easy reach.

"Were your parents divorced?" Lucia asked.

"No, but I divorced my first husband when my older son was an infant. Not my idea," I added after a pause. "Bob disappeared and when I realized he wasn't coming back, it didn't seem like I had much choice."

"My father didn't disappear." Lucia frowned. "But he might as well have. We were hardly ever together, and when I did see him, it felt like he was just doing his duty."

Her hand reached over and tangled in the black curls on Faith's shoulder. The Poodle's tail swished across the floor in response. "The stupid thing is, he didn't want to be bothered with me when I was a child. But now that I'm an adult and perfectly capable of making my own decisions, he seemed to think he had the right to butt in."

"Your mother mentioned something about that," I said.

Lucia nodded. "She's not happy about it either. Especially since there was no reason for Dad to get involved. Trevor and I are happy together. I'd like to think we're going to get married someday. Maybe even someday soon."

I had to smile at the dreamy expression on Lucia's face.

Then she sighed. "Trevor is old-fashioned, he wanted to have my father's permission. Since the two of them had been working together for a year, I thought it would be easy."

"It sounds like it wasn't," I said.

"Not even close. Trevor rehearsed a whole conversation he was going to have with my dad. When it was over, we were supposed to celebrate. But instead of good news, Trevor called and said my father turned him down."

"Did he say why he wouldn't give his permission?" I asked curiously.

Lucia blew out an unhappy breath. "It was stupid stuff, like he thought I was too young to know what I wanted. And Trevor wasn't good enough for me. He said marrying Trevor would hurt my social standing. As if I cared about that."

"Maybe you should have tried talking to him yourself," I said.

"I did. Right after Trevor called, I got in my car and went straight to the store. But here's the awful part." Lucia's lower lip began to quiver. She looked as if she might be blinking away tears. It took a minute for her to gather herself enough to continue.

"That was Monday morning," Lucia said. "Which means I was probably one of the last people to see my father alive. Even worse, our conversation mostly consisted of me screaming at him. I feel horrible about the things I said. I called him a deadbeat dad. What kind of person does that?"

"Someone who's lost her temper and has no idea she won't have a chance to make amends," I said gently. "There's no way you could have known what was about to happen."

"It doesn't matter. I still feel like it was all was my fault. If I hadn't gone storming out of the store . . . if I hadn't left him alone . . . maybe he'd still be alive."

I reached over and laid a hand on her arm. "Or maybe the killer would have attacked you too. Put aside emotion for a moment, and think about it logically. Nothing you said or did caused this terrible thing to happen. It was about your father and the choices he made. That's all."

Lucia lifted her head. She managed a tremulous smile.

"You have absolutely nothing to feel guilty about," I said firmly.

"Maybe you're right." She sniffled. "I hope you're right."

"I am. You need to believe that."

Lucia sniffled again, but she was already looking better. "You're an easy person to talk to." She straightened in her seat and wiped a hand across her cheek. "I bet your students adore you."

"I appreciate the vote of confidence," I said, standing up. It was time to get the room arranged. My first pupil would be arriving shortly. "The truth is, my students adore Faith, which is wonderful. They respect me and my ability to help them. Which is also wonderful. This job is all I've ever wanted to do."

"You're a lucky person," Lucia said. "I hope I can find a career that's as fulfilling as yours."

"I hope you can, too," I told her.

There was a tentative knock, then the door was pushed open. A second-grade girl with big eyes and long blond braids hesitated in the doorway. The stack of books in her arms seemed much too large for her slight frame. "Are you ready for me, Ms. Travis?" she asked in a shy voice.

"I'm always ready for you, Genevieve. Please come in and close the door behind you. I'd like to introduce you to Ms. Willet. She might want to be a teacher, too, someday."

Lucia hopped up out of her seat. "Let me help you with those books," she said. "And maybe you'd like to sit right here next to me?"

After that auspicious beginning, the morning seemed to fly by. Lucia was a natural with the kids. It wasn't just that she engaged with them when they entered the room, she was also able to make them feel at ease as she observed our sessions. Though she remained mostly silent, the few comments she offered were appropriate and well considered.

By the time several hours had passed, I knew I was going to be asking Mr. Hanover if there were any openings on the staff for a classroom aide or assistant teacher. No doubt that outcome was exactly what Julia had in mind all along. Perhaps the knowledge that she'd used our connection to further her own purposes should have bothered me. But years of dealing with Aunt Peg have given me a fondness for women whose ulterior motives often end up being a blessing in disguise.

When my school day ended at one o'clock, Lucia thanked me effusively for my time. She then went to convey her gratitude to Harriet and Mr. Hanover. After I closed up my classroom, Faith and I walked out to the parking lot behind the building. She had a short run while I considered what I'd learned earlier.

My conversation with Lucia had been interesting. Until that morning, the information I'd gathered about Mr. Willet's death felt like little more than a jumbled assortment of facts. Now, suddenly, they were beginning to arrange themselves into a pattern that might make sense. When that happened, I knew who I needed to talk to next.

Faith and I left the school grounds and drove downtown. I parked in a shady spot on Milbank Avenue, a road close to Greenwich Avenue but much less crowded. Once again, Faith would have to wait in the car. Since she wasn't a service dog, she wouldn't be allowed to accompany me where I needed to go.

The Greenwich Police Department was located inside the town's large Public Safety Complex. The group of connected buildings took up nearly an entire block and looked daunting from the outside. This wasn't my first visit, however, so I knew my way around. I went in through the main entrance, gave my name to the receptionist behind the glass, and asked to speak with Detective Young. Then I prepared to wait.

Only a few minutes passed before a young policewoman in a crisp uniform came to escort me to his office. She didn't initiate a conversation, so I didn't either. After making several turns, the woman led me down a corridor I hadn't previously visited. Her soft-soled shoes didn't make a sound as we walked on the linoleum floor, which made my boots seem even louder. I had to hurry along to keep up with her.

"Here we are." She stopped finally, knocked twice, then opened a door. As soon as I entered the room, she pulled the door shut behind me.

Detective Young was seated behind a large desk. He stood up as I came inside, then walked around to shake my hand.

"This is new." I looked around appreciatively. The office was not only bigger than Young's previous space, it also had a second window and a rug on the floor. Two framed commendations hung on the wall above a low file cabinet. "It's nice."

"I'm glad my office meets with your approval." The detective waved me to a chair that was low-slung and surprisingly comfortable. Unfortunately, it also placed me in the position of having to look up at him. I was sure that was intentional.

"I want to talk to you about Gregory Willet's murder," I said, as he reclaimed his much higher chair behind the desk.

"I figured as much. What would you like to tell me?"

Despite what I might want, Detective Young always expected to receive information from me, rather than offer it. I was used to that by now.

I gathered my thoughts for a moment, then said, "I've spoken with a number of people who knew Willet well. His ex-wife and daughter, his landlord, a couple of his neighbors, as well as the man who owns the salon next store."

"Stash Delorean." Detective Young seemed amused by the name.

"Yes, Stash." I smiled with him. "He offered me a manicure."

His hand went up to rub the side of his jaw. "He offered me a shave."

That made me chuckle. "Stash isn't the most subtle guy. But the problem he was having with Willet didn't seem to be worth killing over. Especially since, if Stash is to be believed, the two of them had already worked out an agreement."

Young nodded and waited for me to continue.

"The same problem—not enough motive—is true for the neighbors who were upset about his Chows. And for Len Crater, who owns the property. If a man falls behind in his rent and you kill him for it, how does that help you?"

"It doesn't," Detective Young agreed. I got the impression he was waiting for me to get to the point.

"Which brings me to his family," I said.

"Julia Geist." He stared at me across the top of his desk. "You spoke with her?"

"I did. Twice."

The detective didn't look pleased to hear that. "That's one more audience than I was able to get. Ms. Geist is an influential person in this town. She has friends in high places. We were told to tread lightly."

I was delighted to discover that for once my connections had been better than his. "Julia wanted something from me," I admitted. "Plus, she liked the fact that I'm a teacher."

Young was already sitting up straight in his seat. Even so, I noted the subtle stiffening of his shoulders. "What did she want?"

"Big picture—to be rid of her ex-husband for good. But from me specifically, help in getting her daughter, Lucia, a job at Howard Academy."

He ignored the second part of what I'd said and zeroed in immediately on the first. "How badly did she want to be rid of Willet?"

"Not enough to kill him. At least I don't think so." I hoped I was right about that. "Julia's a very wealthy woman. I suspect she could have paid Willet to get lost, if it came to that. He'd married her for her money, and when they divorced, he received a generous settlement—both alimony and part ownership of the store. Even so, he was now short on funds again. According to both Julia and Lucia, he was trying to work his way back into their lives. Which brings me to my next point."

"Go on."

"Were you aware that Lucia was at Willet's store Monday morning shortly before he was killed? She believes she was the last person he spoke to before he died."

"No." Detective Young growled under his breath. He yanked a pad of paper toward himself and wrote something down. "No one told us that."

"Did you interview her?"

"No, Ms. Geist wouldn't allow it. She said it was unnecessary. Also that Lucia was too upset to talk to us."

"Julia's very protective of Lucia. I'd imagine she cares more about her daughter's well-being than she does about the authorities figuring out what happened to her ex."

He waved a hand in the air, encouraging me to keep talking.

"Lucia wants to marry Willet's assistant, Trevor Pine. For her entire life, she and her father hadn't had a close relationship. But now, inexplicably, Willet felt entitled to have a say in the matter."

"I take it he was opposed?" he asked.

"According to Lucia, vehemently so. Willet forbade Trevor to propose to Lucia. The two men had a fight about it on Monday morning. When Lucia found out, she went storming over to the store to argue with her father too."

"All of this is news to me." Detective Young was disgruntled about that. "Lucia told you that when she left the store, her father was alive?"

"Yes," I said, then added, "of course she did."

Otherwise we'd have been having a very different conversation.

"And you believed her?"

"Yes." Again, I paused. "I think so."

The detective eyed me intently. Like he was trying to decide whether or not I was a reliable witness. I was wondering the same thing. In my mind, Lucia wasn't the guilty party. I was almost sure of that. And now that I'd pretty much ruled out everyone else, I hoped Detective Young would come to the same conclusion I had.

"Trevor Pine," he said softly.

And there it was.

Chapter
Fifteen

"Now what happens?" I asked him.

Detective Young pushed back his chair and stood. "Now you go home and play with your dog."

Reluctantly, I got up too. Just when things were getting interesting, I was being dismissed. "What are you going to do?"

He scrubbed a hand around the back of his neck. "The only thing I can do. Take this new information and send another request up the chain of command, detailing the reasons why it's imperative that we compel Ms. Geist and her daughter to come in for an interview."

"What about Trevor?" I asked. "You don't need permission to talk to him."

"No, but we've already taken his statement once. I'd hate to spook him by going over the same ground again before I've had a chance to confirm what you've told me. Pine said he was nowhere near Willet's store Monday morning. Now you're saying Lucia can place him there. I want to have a sworn statement behind me when I confront him with his own lie."

I supposed that made sense. Although a more gratifying response would have been Detective Young hopping in a police cruiser, turning on the siren, racing to Willet's store, and arresting Trevor Pine. Like they do on TV.

"Okay," I said, trying not to sound disappointed. "Good luck."

I'd reached the door before he spoke. "Melanie?"

I turned back to look at him.

"Thank you."

"You're welcome."

A smiled played around the corners of his mouth. "In case you're interested, there's something you missed."

I'd been reaching for the doorknob. Now my hand stilled. "I'm interested."

"Len Crater doesn't own the real estate that comprises Willet's store and Delorean's salon. Crater Commercial Management is a cover for someone who didn't want their name to appear in connection with the property."

"Who?" Before I'd even uttered the word, I was sure I knew the answer. Of course I did. "Julia Geist."

"Bingo."

"Did Willet know?"

"Possibly. Ms. Geist told me she suspected he'd found out. That was why he'd stopped paying his rent. She said he was always looking for ways to get back at her for divorcing him."

I nodded. "That could also be why he objected to Lucia's marriage to Trevor. Because Julia was delighted with the idea. Or maybe his intention was simply to hold up the proceedings until he'd gotten another payoff."

Detective Young considered the idea. "If that's the case, Willet miscalculated badly."

"He couldn't have known that ahead of time, though," I said. "Either way, it sounds as though that family was well rid of him."

I was back at my car, giving Faith a proper greeting, when my phone rang.

Earlier, Lucia and I had exchanged numbers and the call was from her. I had no idea how long it would take Detective Young to get the okay for more interviews. The thought of Lucia hanging out with Trevor in the meantime made me very uneasy. I wondered if there was a way I could frame a warning that wouldn't tip the detective's hand. But first I needed to see what she wanted.

"Hey, Lucia," I said. "What's up?"

"I'm at the store, and there's something wrong

with Cider. You know a lot about dogs, so I was wondering if you could come and take a look at him?"

The person who knew all about dogs was Aunt Peg. Everything I knew I'd learned from her. My knowledge barely scratched the surface of hers.

"I guess I can do that." I held the phone in one hand and used the other to scratch beneath Faith's chin. If she was unwell, I knew I'd be desperate for help. "Although maybe you should think about taking Cider to a vet."

"I don't know who his vet is. My dad always took care of stuff like that."

"Even so—"

"I don't want to overreact," Lucia broke in. "For all I know, it may be nothing serious. But now that my dad's gone, Cider is the only link to him I have left. Could you just come and see what you think?"

I paused before replying. "Is Trevor there with you?"

"Umm . . . yeah."

"What does he think?"

"He won't say. He doesn't want to be responsible for making a wrong decision. Please, will you help me?"

"Okay," I said. "I'm on my way. I'll be there in ten minutes."

I got Faith resettled in the backseat, then slid behind the steering wheel. I still had my phone out. I sat and stared at it.

On one hand, this shouldn't present a problem. Until now, Trevor and I had had a friendly relationship. No one had accused him of anything yet. There was no reason for him to have any idea about my suspicions. On the other hand, asking me to diagnose an unspecified ailment in a dog I'd only met once, seemed like a pretty odd request.

Another consideration was that Lucia was now in the very situation I'd hoped to warn her about. At least if we were together, there'd be some safety in numbers. And later when I left the store, I would make sure Lucia did too.

Faith sat up on the backseat and poked her nose around the headrest. Now that we were ready to go, she was wondering what was taking so long. Faith was never plagued by indecision. She always knew what was best.

Since I didn't, I was going to hedge my bets.

I turned on my car, pulled out onto the road, then called the Greenwich PD and asked to speak with Detective Young. After a minute, the operator informed me that he was out of his office, but I could leave a message and he'd get back to me.

I waited for the beep, then said, "This is Melanie Travis. Lucia Willet just called me from Willet's store. Trevor Pine is also there. They think something is wrong with Cider." I paused, then clarified. "He's the

Chow. I'm on my way there now. I just thought some-one should know where I am."

Maybe that would be helpful, maybe not. My sec-ond call was to Aunt Peg.

"It's about time I heard from you," she said when she picked up. She had a point, but if I admitted that I'd never hear the end of it.

"I need your help," I said instead. "I'm on my way to Mr. Willet's store. There seems to be a problem with Cider, the Chow."

"What's wrong with him?"

"I don't know. Mr. Willet's daughter, Lucia, thinks I can help."

Aunt Peg snorted under her breath. A not unex-pected response.

"There's also a possibility that the problem is something else entirely," I said.

"Because you think a sick Chow isn't enough to pique my interest?" Aunt Peg retorted. "I assume this has something to do with Gregory Willet's murder?"

"Possibly. Probably. Actually, I'm not sure. But I thought you could be my backup, just in case."

"Backup." Aunt Peg sounded pleased by the pros-pect. "It took you long enough to ask."

I disconnected the call. The sooner Aunt Peg stopped talking, the sooner she could get in her minivan and start driving. If she was home, that meant she was at least twenty minutes away from the store. Then again, Aunt Peg drove like a speed demon even when she wasn't in a hurry. For all I knew, she might beat me there.

For once, I was able to park nearby. As soon as I turned off the car, Faith immediately jumped up. Unfortunately, I had bad news for her again.

"I'm sorry." I reached around from the front seat to cup her muzzle gently between my palms. "I don't have a choice. I don't know what's going on with Cider, and I don't want to expose you to anything if there's a real problem."

Faith wasn't impressed with that speech. She knew I was concerned about something. She tried to press herself forward into my arms. "Not this time," I said. "You stay here and keep an eye out for Aunt Peg."

When I reached the front door of Willet's Pet Supplies, I saw why parking hadn't been an issue. There was a CLOSED sign on the door. Lights were on inside the building, however, and when I pushed the door, it opened easily. I stepped inside and it swung shut behind me.

"Hello?" I called out.

"We're back here." Lucia poked her head out of the storeroom. "Cider's still not doing well."

I skirted between two tall display cases and made my way to the back of the store. Willet's office door was closed, but Lucia was waiting for me across the hall. At first she appeared to be alone. Then I drew near and saw Cider sprawled on the floor behind her.

Lucia quickly motioned me into the room. Cardboard boxes and plastic bins were stacked on one side of the space. Cider's wire crate was on the other side, along with a water bowl and several chew toys. Someone, probably Trevor, had made an effort to see to the dog's comfort. Cider, however, was oblivious.

The dog's eyes were closed, and his tongue protruded from his half-open mouth. He was half on his haunches and half on his side, as if he'd simply collapsed where he was standing. I could see the rise and fall of his chest from where I stood. That was good. I hunkered down beside him for a closer look.

"How long has he been like this?" I asked.

"I don't know." Lucia ran her hands up and down her arms as if she was chilled. "Since I called you. Maybe twelve minutes?"

"What was he doing before he collapsed?" I gently pushed open Cider's lids and looked at his eyes. They were vacant and unfocused. The Chow's breathing had a raspy quality I didn't like.

"Trevor and I were talking. Then he brought Cider back here to put him in his crate. He said Cider just fell down . . ."

"Did you see it happen?"

I rose to my feet. I couldn't diagnose what was wrong with Cider. We needed a vet. But I also needed to figure out what was really going on.

"No." Lucia bit her lip. "I was up front."

"Where's Trevor now?" I asked. "I thought he was with you."

"He is. He was." She nodded toward the closed door across the hall. "He's in the office."

"Doing what?"

She shrugged uneasily. "Work, I guess." Her gaze slid away from mine. Lucia was not a good liar.

"Trevor should be calling a vet. We need to get Cider looked at."

"We can do that," Lucia agreed. "But first you and I need to talk."

"Talk?" I was surprised. *Now?*

Everything about this situation felt off to me. I suspected that Cider had been given some kind of sedative and that he'd wake up on his own eventually. But I certainly didn't know that for sure. And I wasn't about to wait around to find out.

Whatever was going on, however, Lucia looked genuinely worried. Whether it was about the Chow or something else, I had no idea. Which didn't help my comfort level either.

I walked back out to the hallway. Lucia followed me.

"This morning, in your classroom?" she said. Her

voice rose at the end as if she was asking a question. "You need to know that I made a mistake."

"About what?"

"I guess I was confused because so much has happened in the past few days. I got my timing all mixed up. And I think I might have given you the wrong impression."

"Go on," I said.

"Trevor was never in the store on Monday morning. I misspoke about that."

"You misspoke," I repeated, in case she wanted to retract her statement.

Instead, Lucia nodded. "Yes. Trevor doesn't work mornings. So he couldn't have been here. That wouldn't make sense."

Her voice was firmer now. I wondered if Trevor had given her a script to adhere to. Because I didn't believe what she was telling me for a minute.

"So Trevor didn't meet with your father to ask his permission to propose?"

"No, of course not. Like I said, he wasn't even here. It was just . . ." Her voice trailed away. I waited for her to continue. She didn't.

"Just what?" I finally asked.

Lucia swallowed heavily. "Wishful thinking. You know, on my part. I wanted Trevor to propose so I made up this whole scenario in my head where it seemed like it was happening. But now that I think back about it, I had to have been wrong."

Yes, something was definitely wrong. But it wasn't Lucia's original recollection of events. Clearly Trevor had gotten to her and made her change her story. I hated that I didn't know what he was currently doing. A feeling of unease settled over me like a shroud.

"I get how that could happen," I said loudly, in case he could hear us.

Only an idiot would believe that, but Lucia nodded. She looked relieved.

I looked back at Cider. The dog hadn't moved. Even though much of what I could see consisted of hair, he still had to weight more than fifty pounds. "Here's what we're going to do," I said to Lucia. "You and I will find something to use as a stretcher. Between us, we should be able to carry him out to my car so we can take him to a vet."

"We don't need a stretcher." She cast a nervous glance toward the office door. "Trevor can help. He's picked up Cider before. I've seen him do it."

She'd barely finished speaking before the door opened. I guessed that answered my question about whether or not Trevor had been listening to us. He stepped out into the hallway. He ignored Lucia and the Chow on the floor behind us. His eyes came directly to me.

Previously, Trevor had struck me as an appealing

young man. He'd been concerned about Cider, dili-
gent in his duties, and eager to be helpful. I saw none
of those likable qualities in the glare he trained on
me now.

"Hello, Trevor," I said. "It's nice to see you again."

"Is it?" He moved several steps closer. Now he was
standing between me and Lucia. "I knew you were
asking questions about Mr. Willet's death. I even tried
to cooperate. But that was before Lucia and I talked
and I realized you were trying to frame me for what
happened."

Frame him? It was the answers I'd gathered that
had pointed me in his direction.

"That's not at all what I was doing."

"I'm not an idiot," he snapped. "I know what
you're up to. Don't bother denying it. Lucia may be
gullible, but I'm not."

All at once it felt as though Trevor was much too
close. I tried to take a step back, but the wall was
right behind me.

"Maybe we should talk about this," I said. "It
seems there's a discrepancy about where you were
when Willet was killed. You could clear it up for us.
Maybe you have an alibi for the time in question. If
so, you have nothing to worry about."

Lucia looked at Trevor hopefully. Like she still
believed he might be able to utter a few impromptu
words and everything would return to normal. In the

moment, I felt sorry for her. I hated being the person who was about to dash her prospects for marital bliss.

"I don't have to listen to this." Trevor stuck a hand in his pocket. When he withdrew it, his fingers were clasped around a solid object I couldn't immediately identify. Then I heard a small *snick* and a blade appeared. When he held it up to the light, Lucia gasped.

"Trevor!" she shrieked. "What do you think you're doing?"

"I'm getting out of here." His other hand reached out to clasp her upper arm in a viselike grip. "And you're going to help me."

"I most certainly *am not*." Lucia tried to yank her arm away, but Trevor didn't let go.

Instead he lifted the knife until the point of the blade was just beneath her chin, less than an inch away from the sensitive skin. Lucia's eyes opened wide in shock. I was similarly appalled.

Seconds ago, we'd merely been talking. How had things managed to escalate so quickly?

I pressed myself back against the wall and didn't move. I tried not to even breathe. I didn't want to do anything that might upset Trevor. Or make him feel threatened. I wanted the hand that held the knife to remain perfectly still.

"I thought you loved me," Lucia said with a strangled sob. "You said you wanted to marry me."

"I did," Trevor replied. "Marrying you would have set me up for life."

My heart sank. Trevor hadn't even bothered to soften the callous words. I saw the crestfallen look on Lucia's face and felt even worse for her than I had before. Julia had made the mistake of marrying a gold digger, and now Lucia had been about to fall into the same trap.

We all heard the sound of the front door opening at the same time. "Where is everybody?" Aunt Peg called as she came striding into the store. None of us answered. We didn't move a muscle.

Aunt Peg didn't wait for an invitation. She simply kept coming, advancing down the aisle until she reached the hallway. She saw the three of us standing there, like a tableau that was frozen in place.

For a moment, no one said a word. Then the knife, and its ominous position, caught her eye. Aunt Peg scowled ferociously. She drew herself up to her full height and glared at each of us in turn.

"Whatever's going on here, it's not about to happen on my watch," she growled.

Chapter Sixteen

"Who the hell are you?" Trevor snarled. His upheld hand must have been getting tired. I watched it begin to wobble.

"Obviously someone with more sense than you. Now kindly lower that blade before somebody gets hurt."

Aunt Peg was bigger than Trevor, and her presence was twice as commanding. Most people knew better than to stand up to her, especially when she was in a fury, as she most certainly was now. I could see Trevor's resolve begin to waver.

"You can't tell me what to do," he said, sounding like a whiny baby.

Lucia must have thought so too, because I saw her roll her eyes. The jeopardy was still real, but the energy in the room had shifted with Aunt Peg's arrival. Trevor's menacing demeanor was rapidly disintegrating. I could almost see him deflating under her withering glare.

"If you weren't such a ninny, I wouldn't need to," Aunt Peg said sharply. "So, what's your plan? And please don't tell me you don't have one."

"Trevor was just leaving," I said.

"Excellent idea." Aunt Peg stepped to one side. "I recommend we get out of the way and let him get on with it."

Slowly Trevor lowered his hand. He shifted back, loosening his grip on Lucia's arm. Still holding out the knife, he looked around at the three of us as if he was afraid we might decide to rush him.

Fat chance of that. I was pretty sure I could hear the sound of a siren in the distance. Another minute and Trevor Pine would cease to be my problem.

The moment Trevor released Lucia, I grabbed her and hauled her across the narrow hallway. At first she stumbled slightly in surprise. Then she scampered quickly around to my other side. Now I was between her and Trevor. That made both of us feel better.

"I'm leaving now," he announced, then paused, as if he thought Lucia might beg him to stay. Or maybe volunteer to go with him.

Fortunately, Lucia was smarter than that. She simply pointed toward the door and said, "Go."

Trevor looked at her one last time, then scuttled

past Aunt Peg and took off running. He threw the
door open and raced outside. I hoped a police cruiser
was nearby, waiting for him.

Aunt Peg stepped over to where Lucia and I were
standing. Using just the tips of her fingers, she gently
grasped Lucia's chin and tilted it upward. The skin
underneath was smooth and unmarked. Trevor's knife
hadn't made contact. We all sighed with relief.

Then Aunt Peg looked at me. "Now that the stupid
young man is out of the way, we can get to more important things. I believe there's a dog here who needs
my assistance. Where's Cider the Chow?"

Cider was back from his trip to Peg's vet in time for
dinner.

My guess had been correct. The Chow wasn't sick
or injured, he'd merely been sedated by Trevor, who'd
then used Cider's impaired state as an excuse to get
Lucia to summon me to the store. Trevor was desperate for her to retract the things she'd told me earlier.
Obviously his plan had backfired.

When Aunt Peg, Lucia, and I emerged from the
store, we saw that Trevor had already been detained
by the police. His arrest was made official later that
afternoon. Aunt Peg said I should have been suspicious of him from the start. She maintained that only
someone whom the Chow already knew would have
had an opportunity to harm Mr. Willet.

Trevor Pine's lawyer entered a plea of temporary insanity. He's claiming that the threat of losing Lucia caused Trevor to become unhinged and act in a way he never would have otherwise. It remains to be seen what the court, and a jury, will make of that. Lucia and I are both willing to testify about Trevor's real reason for wanting to marry her, if it becomes necessary.

Much to Lucia's delight, Cider now belongs to her. The Chow is settled in his new home, and he's become the dog she always wanted.

"How does Julia feel about that?" I asked. Her comments about hairy beasts with big teeth were still fresh in my mind.

"She's learning to adapt. There's been so much upheaval in both our lives recently that she's willing to cut me a little slack. Plus, I think she feels guilty that she was so very wrong about Trevor." Lucia looked downcast. "As was I."

"You're young, and you were in love," I said. "It's true what they say about rose-colored glasses. Emotion prompts lots of people to make mistakes."

"I'm just glad the whole experience is behind me," she replied. "I'm looking forward to what's ahead."

Lucia had an upcoming meeting with Mr. Hanover, courtesy of Harriet. I hoped the headmaster would feel as positive about her prospects as I did. And if by some chance he didn't, I was sure Julia would get to work again, pulling more strings until she'd settled things to her satisfaction.

I later heard that Julia also met with Stash about his upcoming lease renewal. She ended up offering him a long-term lease at favorable terms. In exchange, Stash promised to personally cut and style her hair as long as they did business together. That seemed like a good deal to me.

Harriet and I wrapped up the Thanks for Giving fundraiser just in time for the Thanksgiving holiday. The event was an enormous success. Not only did the school raise a large sum of money for its scholarship fund, but having our students engage with Greenwich shopkeepers earned us a significant amount of goodwill locally.

The sixth-grade class collected the greatest number of pumpkin spice tokens. They were named winners of the treasure hunt, and a party was held in their honor. During the event, all the students who had participated were given the opportunity to exchange their tokens for prizes.

Harriet and I were in charge of refreshments. Naturally we chose pumpkin spice as our theme. With autumn just about over, everyone was delighted to have a chance to savor the seasonal flavor one last time. Our cookies, muffins, and ice cream were a huge hit.

Once the fundraiser was behind me, Thanksgiving was next on my agenda. Aunt Peg was coming to our house for dinner. She'd volunteered to bring dessert. I was cooking the rest of the meal. By late morning, I had a twelve-pound turkey in the oven. That left plenty of time for me to work on my side dishes.

Then Aunt Peg arrived, and all my careful planning went out the window. Overnight, we'd had our first snowstorm of the year. The air outside was crisp and cold, and we had six inches of snow on the ground.

A frigid blast entered the house along with Aunt Peg. She stood in our front hall surrounded by five excited dogs and two excited children, and clapped her mitten-clad hands to get everyone's attention.

"Who's ready for a snowball fight?" she roared.

"Me!" Kevin cried.

"Me, too," Davey chimed in. "But I don't want to be on Mom's team."

"Hey!" I said. "What's the matter with my team?"

"You lose," Kevin told me sadly. "Every time."

"I do not." Well, maybe sometimes. But that was just the law of averages. And the fact that I could hardly vanquish my own children. Sam had no such qualms. He was known as the winner in the family.

"Fine." I pointed to each of my sons in turn. "You two can be on Dad's team. Aunt Peg and I will take you on."

Aunt Peg looked taken aback by that development. Her competitive streak was a mile wide. She hated to lose at anything. "We will?"

"We will," I said firmly. Tough luck for her. She was the one who'd come up with the idea.

It took ten minutes to get everyone suited up. When Kevin thought he was ready, I added a scarf around his neck and made sure his rubber boots were securely fastened. By the time I was finished, he was so bundled up he could barely move.

Sam said under his breath to me, "You know that's not going to save you, right?"

"It won't need to. I'm depending on your innate sense of decency for that. Who are you going to aim at out there, your loving wife or a woman who's old enough to be your mother?"

All five dogs followed us outside. Faith remained on the deck, but Eve, Tar, Augie, and Bud joined us in the snow-covered yard. The snow was slightly wet and perfect for packing. I was building up an arsenal of snowballs when Aunt Peg picked one up and let fly. It hit Sam squarely in the chest.

He looked surprised when a shower of icy flakes exploded upward into his face. Then he grinned, scooped up a handful of snow, and prepared to retaliate. "Oh, it's on," he said.

The yard quickly turned into a melee of barking dogs, flying snowballs, and shrieking children. Or maybe that was mostly me. Thanks to Aunt Peg, she and I were holding our own. Then Bud got into my snowball supply and destroyed half of it. Kevin accidentally tripped his older brother, and they both went down in a heap.

Sam, meanwhile, was reloading. He cocked back his arm and drew a bead on me.

I held up my hands in a gesture of surrender. "Truce!"

"Truce?" Aunt Peg glared at me in outrage. "We were winning!"

"I think it was a tie," I said.

"I'll take a tie," Sam agreed.

The boys didn't get a vote. They were still rolling around in the snow, along with Tar and Augie, who'd come to join them. They were all going to be cold and wet by the time they were done.

"I'm not agreeing to a tie," Aunt Peg announced.

The snowball glistened in Sam's cupped palm. He shifted his aim slightly, then threw it. I ducked, but it wasn't coming at me. It flew past my head and knocked off Aunt Peg's hat.

"Care to reconsider?" Sam asked.

Davey looked up and crowed, "Good one, Dad!"

"That was unfair," Aunt Peg said.

"I think not." Sam was grinning again. The top of his jacket was unzipped, and his eyelashes glittered with a coating of ice. He looked wonderful. "All's fair in love and snowball fights."

"Then I guess it's a tie," Aunt Peg decided. "Now what's for dinner?"

"Turkey!" Kevin giggled. He stood up and brushed off his pants. "It's Thanksgiving."

"What's for dessert?" I asked Aunt Peg. She'd been carrying a box when she arrived, but I didn't know what was inside.

"Pumpkin spice pie," she said. "You're going to love it."

PUMPKIN SPICE COOKIES

Harriet and Melanie served these cookies at the party to celebrate the success of the Howard Academy fundraiser. Flavorful and small enough to pop in your mouth, they're the perfect treat to accompany a hot beverage on a brisk autumn afternoon.

Ingredients

2½ cups flour
2 tsps. baking soda
2 tsps. ginger
2 tsps. cinnamon
¾ tsp. nutmeg
1 tsp. salt
½ cup butter (softened)
1 cup sugar
½ cup pumpkin puree
¼ cup molasses
½ tsp. vanilla extract
1 egg

Instructions

Combine all the dry ingredients (except sugar) in a small bowl.

Mix together the sugar and butter.

Add the molasses, pumpkin puree, vanilla extract, and egg, and continue to mix.

Slowly stir in the dry ingredients.

Cover and refrigerate the dough for at least an hour.

Preheat the oven to 350 degrees.

Line a cookie sheet with parchment paper.

Shape the dough into medium-sized balls and place them, spaced, on the cookie sheet.

Bake for 11–12 minutes.

Tips:

Do not substitute pumpkin pie filling for the pumpkin puree.

Feel free to play around with the combination of spices.

Both light and dark molasses work with this recipe.

For sweeter cookies, before baking, roll the balls of dough in granulated sugar.